# JANIE

Janie is a champion skier. Young and beautiful, she is continually in the news, while Roy is a struggling writer, obscure and lonely. He falls in love with her, but realises that she is far above him. Then, abruptly, the situation changes. Janie suffers an accident and slips out of the news, but Roy makes the headlines when the film rights of one of his books are sold . . . Can Janie and Roy overcome their differences and find lasting happiness?

# IAIN TORR

◆

# JANIE

*Complete and Unabridged*

# LINFORD
*Leicester*

First published in Great Britain in 1974 by
Robert Hale & Company
London


First Linford Edition
published 2008
by arrangement with
Robert Hale Ltd
London

British Library CIP Data

MacKinnon, Charles Roy
Janie.—Large print ed.—
Linford romance library
1. Love stories
2. Large type books
I. Title
823.9'14 [F]

ISBN 978–1–84782–265–9

Published by
F. A. Thorpe (Publishing)
Anstey, Leicestershire

Set by Words & Graphics Ltd.
Anstey, Leicestershire
Printed and bound in Great Britain by
T. J. International Ltd., Padstow, Cornwall

This book is printed on acid-free paper

# 1

The year in which Jane Lyon won the women's world cup for skiing was a bonus year for the sports commentators. Janie was virtually unknown, she was British and the British were in need of a boost for their sporting prestige that year — and, human interest to end all human interest stories, she was stone deaf. She had been born deaf. This pretty gold-haired twenty-year-old had lived in Switzerland with her English parents for twelve years, skied like a dream, was the most outstanding downhill skier anyone had ever seen, broke three world records in one season, and she had never skied competitively before.

They went wild over her, and there was plenty to write about. Her father had been a successful machine tool manufacturer until his health played him up and he decided to go to live in Switzerland. He had invested in a hotel at Lenk in the Bernese Oberland, and there the Lyon family had lived for the past dozen years. Janie skied at Lenk and Adelboden, but most years she went to Zermatt and Saas Fee for the ski touring. She loved cross-country skiing. It was only when she showed up at Murren one year that she was spotted by Franz Bruggman, who had won more skiing Olympic Gold Medals than anyone else and was virtually a Swiss national hero. Bruggman swore that he had been talking to her for fully ten minutes before he discovered that she was deaf.

'Please don't turn your head when you're speaking,' she had said. 'I'm deaf.'

She said it in beautiful German. She also spoke French and of course English. It was marvellous. On television they showed clips of her great world-beating downhill run almost as often as they showed the Prime

Minister making speeches. Predictably she became Sportswoman of the Year, and Princess Anne talked to her on television, and it was practically impossible to believe that this vivacious girl was deaf, had always lived in a strange silent world unknown to other people, a world into which sound had never penetrated.

It was when she came to England for the award that Roy Monro really noticed her for the first time. It hadn't been Roy's good year. There had been the messy divorce, messy because his wife was unnecessarily greedy and had claimed more alimony than he could really afford. He was a writer and as such he had no set level of income. Of course the lawyers had averaged out his earnings and come up with a figure that was acceptable, but Gertrude had been bitter about it, and what had started off as an amicable thing was somehow made ugly and unpleasant. It left a nasty taste, and to make things worse he had had a bad off-period during which nothing seemed to turn out right. There were three novels which he had started but never contrived to complete. Suddenly towards the end of the summer everything came right and he swung back into his old style, writing hard and fast for about five hours a day, five hours which exhausted him emotionally, but left him time to go walking in the afternoons.

He lived in rather a dilapidated cottage not far from Little Malvern. He had given their smart Gloucestershire house and its contents to Gertrude, whose gratitude consisted of the complaint that he had said he was going to have the garage re-roofed and hadn't done it, would he kindly give her £100 to have it done? He had refused. He was more concerned with trying to get someone to do work in the new cottage, but it was not easy. Everyone was busy, it seemed. Roy himself was no good with his hands, and after one or two half-hearted attempts to repair things, he gave up. His study was warm and comfortable, and so was his bedroom, and the rest did not matter greatly. He could afford to wait. He would be forty-six later that year. They had been divorced a few days after their twenty-first wedding anniversary.

They soon found out who he was in Little Malvern. Roy Monro's books sold reasonably well, they were stocked in all libraries, sold in many bookshops, and appealed to a wide readership. He wrote about Regency England and was a considerable authority on that period although he never aired his learning except in his novels. It did not take people long to discover that the minor celebrity who had bought Evanton Cottage was also a recluse and did not welcome intrusion. Even the vicar met with a frosty reception. It was not that Roy was rude — he simply took no interest, said nothing, and waited patiently for people to go away.

Quite a number of people swore they would never buy another of his books, with that aggrieved sense of injured rectitude invariably worn by inquisitive people who have been snubbed. Of course almost all of them got their books from the library anyway, and what it did was to create a mild interest on the part of others. His sales were not affected one way or the other — indeed, as he well knew, if Worcestershire had disappeared completely off the face of the map overnight, it would not affect his standard of living at all. Most of his sales came from the U.S.A.

On the night of the presentation of the Sportswoman award he lay awake in bed for a long time doing what he had not done recently — thinking of someone else. It intrigued him that the girl was deaf. It also intrigued him that she had such a pleasant voice. How could that be? Had her parents trained her so that the pitch and tone were right? Was it a lucky accident? The girl herself could not know how she sounded. Indeed, he realised with astonishment, the word 'sound' was just that to her — a word. A meaningless word. How did you describe sound to someone deaf? How did you tell them what music was? What sort of lonely still world was it they inhabited?

At the same time as he was asking all these questions he could visualise the radiantly healthy freckle-faced girl in the attractive dress, with golden hair and a sunny smile. It was only the following morning that he realised what had happened. He had fallen in love in the way of a schoolboy — foolishly, unreasonably, hopelessly. He had never even seen this girl in the flesh, only on a TV screen. She was quarter of a century younger than he was, full of youth and innocence, with the promise of life unsullied. He was old, tired, rather cynical, and there was no promise left in his life. He had his thing to do, he did it tolerably well, and so it would be until they buried him six feet under the sod.

He tried to dismiss the whole ridiculous affair. He turned to a new novel which he had roughly plotted, one about a servant girl. Suddenly he began to write with a controlled savagery that startled even him. The book rolled off his typewriter in record time, took very little editing, and when he had re-typed it he felt as though he had been through a wringer. He posted it off and treated himself to dinner at a little Herefordshire pub where the food was remarkably good.

For the first time he was uncomfortably aware of being alone in the world. He never heard from Gertrude — did not wish to hear from her either. That was all in the past. His only contact with the outside world was Doris Ormonde, his editor. Doris and the television. He didn't even take a daily newspaper nowadays. He promised to change it all, as he sat eating a very fine steak accompanied by mushrooms and ratatouille. It was for the ratatouille that he came here — he could get steak and mushrooms in half a dozen other good restaurants, but not like this.

He ordered another bitter lemon and

decided that he must come to terms with life. It was unhealthy skulking in his shack, avoiding people, getting a silly crush on a young girl who lived in Switzerland, whom he would never meet — for all the world like some giddy girl falling in love with a pop idol. He was intelligent, mature, and his work was improving slowly but surely. It was time to stop feeling sorry for himself.

Next day, buoyed by a new interest in life, he traded in his car for a new one, bought a new blazer and two new pairs of slacks, and wrote a number of letters which he had been evading for the past four months or more. He did some more shopping in the afternoon, browsed round the bookshop and had a few words with the manager about one or two reference works he wanted to order, which was really a sop to local feelings as normally he got all his books from a celebrated bookseller in Oxford. He had tea in *Patty's* where he was seen and recognised, and went home feeling virtuous. Next day he made several telephone calls and finally found someone who could come to redecorate three rooms, and who knew a carpenter and electrician who would do minor jobs. He felt ridiculously pleased with life.

Winter was approaching again, and he decided that this year he would go abroad at Christmas. It had been a mistake to spend last Christmas alone in England. It had merely served to make him miserable on Christmas Day and Boxing Day. This year he would have a holiday. He decided to go to Switzerland. He would go to Davos and skate. In his youth, in London, he had belonged to Queens Ice Club and had skated regularly and fairly well. It would be fun to try it again after all these years — how many? Nearly twenty-five he supposed. He'd left London at twenty-one, bought his first cottage in the country, and begun to write with incredible optimism for one so young and inexperienced.

He remembered those war years in London, and the immediate post-war years. He was lucky he had never had to go into the Army to do national service like others had done. He had been in hospital with rheumatic fever when they sent for him, which meant that he was temporarily unfit. For some peculiar reason they never tried to call him up after that, although he lived in constant expectation of an official letter in the post. It did not come. In 1949 he left London and if they tried to find him after that, he knew nothing of it. He had lived in the country, met Gertrude at a party in Cirencester, married her, and bought a better house when his sales justified it. Now she had the house and he was back to a cottage. Well, he would go back to skating too. It would be fun.

A local travel agent made the arrangements for him and for several days he kept himself amused by kitting himself out.

One day Doris Ormonde telephoned.

'Roy, when are you coming to London?'

'Who's going to pay my fare?' he asked mildly.

'No use to plead poverty with me. I know to a cent how much you make.'

'Don't remind me,' he laughed. 'I am an eternal supplicant at your feet for my daily bread!'

'That's what I'm calling about,' she chuckled. 'Your latest effort. *Miss Prudence*. We don't like the title at all, but we do like the book. Not only do we like it, but Dinwoodie's in New York have twenty thousand dollars advance says they like it.'

'That's nice.'

'Don't worry, it will make a lot more than that. I'm not proposing to argue with Dinwoodie's because I know you don't bother too much about the advances as long as you can pay the rent.'

'That's right,' he agreed. 'In the long run it's how many copies they sell that counts, not how much they pay in advance.'

'This one will go like wildfire. I'm sure of it. I couldn't put it down, Roy. What got into you?'

'I don't know. It only took me fifteen days to write it.'

'I knew you were fast, but not that fast.'

'I slaved at it all day. Of course it took another month to tidy it up, but the initial writing was exactly fifteen days. I just had to get it out of my system and it came away with a wild rush.'

'I hope you are going to have lots more wild rushes. We'll all be millionaires. I'll send you the usual contract. What advance do you want?'

This was something unusual in their relationship, asking him how much he wanted. She guessed what the answer would be.

'Oh nothing, not if Dinwoodie's are paying all that much.'

'They are paying half on signature and half on publication.'

'Their first ten thousand will go a

long way. I'll collect from you *after* publication.'

'What I like about you is that you aren't greedy.'

'You're wrong,' he pointed out with a laugh. 'I'm thinking of the taxman. I don't want everything at once. I like to spread the jam over a year or two. For God's sake don't send me any more money before April. I've had enough for this year.'

'I wish I had your problems,' she commented.

'Doris dear, there is another angle. The more I get the more I spend. Right now the alimony is covered, and so are all my living expenses. I've got plenty left over for my other needs; so why collect a whole lot more?'

'I thought you were having that house done up.'

'Cottage, not house. Four rooms, loo and kitchen. It's tiny. I *am* having it done up. In fact they've started. It's only going to cost £250 all told, and I thought I'd spend another couple of

14

hundred at the Cheltenham auctions to get a few nice bits of old furniture.'

'Then what's to stop you coming to London for lunch?'

'That's a hell of a way to go for lunch,' he replied with a grin. 'It's an idea. I could do a little shopping. I want to get down to more work soon. When and where?'

'Monday at lunchtime,' she replied promptly. 'Meet me at Simpson's at twelve-thirty. All right?'

'Fine Doris. Thanks for calling about the book.'

'Thanks for reminding me — the title! For heaven's sake think up something decent.'

'I will. I knew you'd ask me, but I had to give it some sort of a name, didn't I? I'll think of something else between now and Monday.'

'We may just possibly have a paperback deal ready for you by then.'

'Don't hang up. I like your conversation.'

'I told you, it's a good book. Why

didn't you do one like it before?'

He paused and thought. It was a good question. What was it that had got him so steamed up that the book poured out so angrily? He usually had a certain tenuous control over what he wrote, but not this time.

'I don't really know how it happened,' he admitted.

'Something's happened to you. You aren't in love are you?' she joked.

'Don't be gruesome. One divorce was enough.'

'Sorry, I didn't realise you were sensitive.'

'I'm not. Dammit Doris, why couldn't I be a publisher's editor like you instead of a miserable worm-eaten writer.'

'Worm eaten?' she queried, surprise in her voice.

'We're all worm infested, or we wouldn't do this. There's no cure for it. You can go mad or you can commit suicide, but you can't change. I had my chance when I was twenty.'

'What chance was that?'

'I never told you. It was when I got my N.S.A. silver for ice dancing, some fellow offered me a job in an ice show. I could have been a big star of show biz by now.'

'Or an elderly chorus boy wishing you could write.'

He laughed.

'True oh queen. There is nothing in this world more transitory or more misleading than physical accomplishment.'

'Transitory yes. Misleading how?'

'The super sportsman in real life is probably not a sportsman at all. He's probably mean as all hell and you'd hate to live next door to him. Cardboard heroes all of them, who fade away with middle age.'

'My, aren't you philosophical? Is this another book hatching?'

'When did I ever write that sort of rubbish? Who's paying for this call?'

'Your wealthy publisher, Gerald Mance.'

'Then we'd better hang up, hadn't we?' Roy suggested. 'See you Monday.

You'll recognise me easily. I'm the good looking one in the new blazer.'

★ ★ ★

Roy Monro was one of the few writers whom Doris Ormonde really liked as a person. He had begun his writing career with Mance's at a time when she was desperately unhappy, eighteen years ago just when her husband had died and she had gone back to work. At that time he was an unknown writer, scraping along not too uncomfortably on what he earned. He had been writing contemporary light humour and it was Doris who suggested to him, after learning that his hobby was reading history, that he try a historical novel. He had written his first Regency book then, and it had been a good one. There had been nothing bad since, although some books were obviously more good than others.

He was unpretentious, amusing, reasonably hard working, always surprised that his books earned money, and always ready and willing to listen to her. It was this last trait which made him so endearing. He was astonishingly modest and unassuming. She had gone through a stage, near the beginning of their relationship, of thinking she was in love with him, despite the fact that he was nine years younger than herself. Why not? Did a woman *have* to love an older man? Men certainly didn't care much for older women — most of them anyway. It had worn off but it had left a deep affection. He was 'her' author in a way none of their other authors were.

She saw him a second before he saw her, and then he stood up, smiling. He looked quite fit, and certainly smart. He dressed well — not expensively or ostentatiously, but nicely — and he had a good figure. He was looking his age, though, as if he hadn't been sleeping properly.

'Hullo Doris. Right on time as always, and very lovely.'

'No flattery please.'

'You do look nice,' he insisted. 'What will you have to drink?'

Another bond between them was that they had both given up smoking and drinking about the same time and had written one another occasional progress reports. It was all nearly eighteen years ago, but it was something else which linked them together.

'Tomato juice please.'

'And another for me,' Roy said to the waiter. 'Make it two. We'll order in five minutes.'

She put down her handbag and gloves and smiled at him.

'You look tired.'

'Do I? I suppose I am a little. It isn't work.'

'Worry?'

'Nothing and nobody to worry about except myself,' he answered without the least trace of self pity. 'Age perhaps.'

'You're a young man.'

'Forty-six next week. It scares me.'

So that's what it is, she thought with quick pity. He's realised he isn't going to live for ever. It comes to us all in middle age and it's hell.

'Wait till you're my age, my boy,' she told him briskly. 'I've only got forty-six years to go before the Queen sends me a telegram on my hundredth birthday.'

'He laughed. 'You're never stuck for a reply are you?'

'Let's order,' she said, and they studied the menus. They talked about books for a time — he was interested in sociology these days, and had been reading Robert Ardrey again.

'I wish I could believe in religion,' he remarked when the lobster bisque had been served. 'It all seems so futile. Life I mean. It must be nice to be able to believe in life after death. It's a silly theory of course — untenable — but comforting.'

'You'll get over the hump, Roy.'

'Does it show badly?'

'Not badly, but I know what's wrong. We all reach the same stage. You feel life is over, don't you?'

'Isn't it? The things I can't do any

more.' He looked momentarily miserable. 'I wish I'd paid more attention to life twenty years ago. I can't even remember properly now. I wish I could.'

'You should be thinking of the future, not the past.'

'What future, Doris? At my age, what's the future? Bigger sales, more income tax, more loneliness? Perhaps a more expensive coffin when I die — except that I want to be cremated if there's anyone around to bother about my wishes.'

'It's a pity you and Gertrude had no children.'

'Pity my foot. I wouldn't have divorced her if there had been a child, and that would have been worse. My trouble is that I'm a middle-aged failure. I don't mean I'm poor, just that I'm spiritually bankrupt. I'm Mr. Nobody going Nowhere. And I'm *not* sorry for myself but I *am* sorry to be talking about me. Tell me about the book.'

'Have you found a name for it?' she

asked, going along with his mood.

'Oh yes, three or four.' He took an envelope from his pocket and handed it to her. 'They're in there. Take your pick and if you don't like any, throw them back at me. There's no mad rush yet, is there?'

'Not for a few weeks. We've got a paperback deal for you. They insist on paying an advance.'

'Keep it small. How much?'

'They suggested a thousand pounds.'

'Make it a quarter of that. Try to stall them off till April.'

'You've got a thing about income tax, haven't you?'

'I don't need more than five thousand a year, but there may be years when I make less, so I like to know there's always money to come. This year if you remember there was that sudden windfall from that American TV company. I've had nearly six thousand out of you and there's still a lot of that in the bank. Let's keep things on an even keel.'

'What would you do if you wrote a best seller?' she asked laughing.

'God knows. The thought of paying three quarters of my earnings to a Government as inefficient as this one would drive me insane. To any Government in fact. I suppose I'd go to Switzerland.'

As he spoke she saw a strange fleeting expression on his face and wondered what had caused it.

'You wouldn't be the first,' she told him.

'No, nor the last, but oddly enough I like it in England. I don't want to go abroad. America maybe. I loved that last lecture tour. I wouldn't go there to live, though. This is home.'

'How's the cottage?'

'Improving. By the time I go, it will be just fine. You must come and visit me.'

'Go where?'

'I didn't tell you. I'm off to Davos, skating.'

He told her about his holiday, which

would cover three weeks from mid December to the end of the first week in January.

'It sounds fun,' she said enviously.

'It will be a change. I haven't been away for a proper holiday for a couple of years now. I shall come back chock full of ideas for books and work like a dingbat for the next twelve months.'

'When did you last skate?'

'When I was twenty-one. Long time ago. I'm only going to potter about on the edge of the ice and try to recapture my lost youth. Call it a sentimental journey.'

'Is it wise? All this looking over your shoulder, I mean?'

'I didn't mean it seriously. I can't look back at Davos — I've never been there before. I always wanted to go, you know, but I had no money in those days. Isn't it funny how we have to wait so long to realise our ambitions? It won't be the same now as it would have been then. Suppose I'd gone to Davos when I was twenty-one, instead of buying that cottage at Cerney Wick and taking a chance on writing? Who knows what would have happened. I'd never have met Gertrude. I might never have been a writer. I could have been a lot happier.'

'Roy, you're my favourite person and you know it. So will you stop all that stupid nonsense about what might have been? If you want another American lecture tour to soothe your ego I'll get in touch with Dinwoodie's. I'm sure it can be done.'

'Sorry Doris. It wasn't that. My ego is all right. I'm just moody.'

'I can see that.'

'I feel sort of dirty, somehow. Not pornographic dirty,' he added with a boyish grin. 'Just shopsoiled. I wish I could get back my innocence, recapture that spirit I had when I saw the world as a decent place.'

'Isn't it a decent place?'

'You know as well as I do that nothing is what it seems,' he shrugged.

They ate in silence for a time.

'Any plans for the next book?' she asked cautiously.

'I thought of writing one in modern English,' he laughed.

'Like what?'

'Like I hear on TV every day until I'm weary and faint from it. I shall call it *Jargowocky*. I wrote the first paragraph for you. Hang on.'

He fished out his wallet and extracted a folded sheet of paper which he handed to her. She scanned it quickly before laughing.

'The Prime Minister looked round the House before continuing,' it began.

''At this point in time, in fact, the grass roots support right across the board, had been made absolutely clear to the mass media, and opens up opportunities for dialogue and areas for agreement. It will be possible now to devise a formula resulting in swingeing changes by means of which a realistic accommodation can be found. In fact, you know, that is what it's all about. It is the name of the game.'

'As he paused there was enthusiastic applause.'

She looked up at him. 'When did you write this?' she asked.

'Last night, during a very well-known television programme which I invariably watch, on which two politicians spoke for about fifteen minutes. I jotted down every jarring jargon phrase and strung them together. It has about as much meaning as anything in real life.'

'Can I keep it?'

'Of course. I don't want it.'

'Thank you.' She put it in her handbag.

'That's what assaults our ears and our intelligence daily. The trouble is that we do it ourselves. I find myself writing it. How much better to write the commercials, where no such vagueness is allowed. 'Test king size Dazzle. Hot wash or cool, it banishes halitosis and make your teeth really sparkle . . . just like real ones.' I'm sure I'd do well in the ad game.'

'You might even survive a single day,' she agreed.

They had disposed of the buttered asparagus, and the mushroom omelettes with the delicious tomatoes stuffed with paté and egg yolk, and they were studying the formidable list of sweets.

'Roy,' she said abruptly, 'why don't you give up that cottage at Malvern and come to London? You're far too young and good looking to bury yourself.'

'What?' He stared at her.

'You heard. I think you brood too much in the country. I know it's fashionable to prefer country to city, but you're alone now, and think of what you're missing? There's so much goes on in London.'

'Where would I live? I'd have to write a book a month to survive. It's expensive.'

'It isn't that bad, and you know it.'

'Nothing will get me back to London. I was raised here, went to school here, and had a job in an office here for a time. I was glad to get away.'

'Oh well, it was an idea. You're really a nice person, but who knows it?

Nobody ever has a chance to meet you.'

'For an editor you cover a lot of territory.'

'Are you warning me off? she asked.

'No Doris.' He gave her a look of warm affection. 'I'm far too fond of you. You're right. I must get out more. London isn't the answer. I'd never work here. I'll have to reorganise my life, that's all.'

'You don't mind my speaking out of turn?' she asked.

'Never. It's done me good just having lunch with you. I think I'll stay in town tonight. Will you come to a show with me?'

She hesitated for a brief moment and then nodded.

'All right. Do you have a hotel?'

He shook his head.

'Then I'll call the office and get them busy on it. You won't find it easy. What about clothes?'

'I've only got what I stand up in. Does it matter?'

She hesitated and made a decision.

'You'd better stay at my flat then. There's a spare bedroom.'

'That's kind of you, but what about the neighbours?'

'I'm too old to attract that sort of gossip. Anyway,' she added truthfully, 'it would be flattering.'

The fact was that the neighbours hardly ever saw one another; and no hotel would really feel happy about a customer without even a toothbrush. Apart from which, she had not really found out what was wrong. Something specific was upsetting him, and she wanted to know what it was. Perhaps if they were together she'd find out.

# 2

Despite the months that had passed since she astonished the world by becoming women's world champion skier, Janie found it difficult to adjust to the new circumstances. She had been asked to write her story for the newspapers, to write a book, to appear on television panel games, to appear in television commercials — indeed if money had been a problem, it would have been solved. It could all have been flattering and even amusing but for one thing — the fuss people made about her deafness. She had an uneasy feeling that had she not been deaf there would have been a lot less fuss, that it was for her handicap rather than for herself that she was sometimes admired.

The strange silent world in which she lived was not quite so strange as some people thought, for she had known no other. She had been born deaf. She was sorry for people who started off normal and became deaf; sorrier still for the blind. She had tried to explain this to a journalist but his editor had killed that part of the story because he did not think it was good copy. It interfered with the image he was creating.

There was a dreamlike unreality about the whole business. Of course she had always been a natural skier and completely unafraid. At Lenk they said she was the fastest thing anyone had ever seen on skis but they did not mean it literally, or translate it into top class competition terms. It took the meeting at Murren with Franz Bruggman to transform the potential into reality, and even then Janie herself was not convinced. She admired Bruggman and was willing to humour him, but she did not expect to do well. Yet after months of private coaching she had gone right to the top in her first season, against all probabilities; achieving the impossible as more than one sports writer put it.

She sat with her father, having dinner at the Café Royal after an early appearance on television, and wished she were home.

'Something wrong darling?' he asked his daughter noticing the look in her eye.

'A little bit fed up,' she answered. 'I wish I hadn't agreed to ski again this year. I want to stop. I also wish I hadn't agreed to this TV appearance.'

'I see.' Jack Lyon looked round the room before replying. He liked the Café. He often came here when he visited London, which was about three times a year, usually alone for neither Janie nor Susan her mother particularly enjoyed these trips away from Lenk. 'You're committed now, but if you want to make this your last year you'd better announce the fact as soon as this season is over. Some people are going to be disappointed. You're now Britain's leading Olympic hope. Everyone thinks you'll get the gold.'

'That's not for another two years. I

don't know why, but there's no fun left in it.'

'Are you sure you aren't running away from something?'

She looked at him and smiled, that smile he knew so well. He was extraordinarily proud of her.

'I don't think so Jack. I get so little time to myself now and there are so many outside distractions, like these television appearances. I enjoyed it in the very beginning but people always think of me as some sort of freak. I don't want to be a freak.'

'You aren't,' he assured her. 'I know how it is. Sometimes I get mad at the way they drag in your deafness.'

Looking at them talking together nobody would have guessed that she was deaf. Few people realised the hard work that went into lip reading or the constant practice in speaking needed to produce that clear, pleasant voice. Deafness brought its own particular problems. for many avenues were automatically closed to her. Fortunately she was a natural athlete and equally fortunately she was adept at languages. That kept her busy. Although she had no job, nor career, her life was a busy one.

It was the future which posed the problems. Where was she going? She herself had no idea. At the moment she often helped in the hotel and Jack had indicated that he would consider selling his machine-tool business, which he still owned and controlled from long range, and investing everything in the tourist business in Switzerland. If that happened it would virtually mean living in Switzerland permanently, and Janie had not made up her mind about that yet. So matters hung in the balance. There was no urgency about anything.

Jack was not surprised to hear her speak of giving up. The initial intense pride he and Susan had felt at her success had worn off. They were just a little bit tired of reporters, of endless telephone calls, and most of all tired of the flow of letters from admirers. There were proposals of marriage, begging letters, so-called 'business' offers, requests for autographed photographs, passionate declarations of love, in addition to a lot of genuine letters from followers of the sport who simply wrote to congratulate Janie. The daily post had been a bit of a nightmare. If she won again this year there would undoubtedly be another build-up. The worst of it was that one had to read them, or at least start to read them. Some called for a reply. Not many, but some.

He still remembered vividly the one, written in a spidery hand, rather a wandering incoherent letter of congratulation, which had been signed Kristian Kekkonen. It was Franz Bruggman, on a brief visit to Lenk, who had recognised the signature of the Finnish senile invalid who had once been the greatest skier the world had known — sixty years ago. The letter, which had almost been thrown out, was now framed. Janie had written back charmingly, two more letters had been exchanged, and then had come word that Kekkonen was dead. His granddaughter wrote to say that in his last months the letters from Janie had meant more to him than anything in the world. So, you had to read through it all. That was Susan's job, bless her. She was the censor of the family, sorting out the wheat from the chaff.

'It won't be too bad,' Jack told her with a reassuring smile. 'Next week you'll be training again and the months will pass quickly once you get into the swing of it. It's the prospect which is so daunting.'

Janie nodded. She knew that it was the truth.

'I'll still be glad when it is all over. I'll be glad to get home too. London is too crowded for me.'

'You're just a small-town girl,' Jack laughed.

'That's right,' she agreed placidly.

A lot of people recognised her now, and a lot more who did not recognise her still stared for she was an eye-catching person. She wore a red dress this evening, which set off nicely her white-gold hair, cut short off the shoulder. She had a tanned, healthy look quite out of place in the late autumnal London. One commentator had dubbed her 'Doris Day on skis' and it was not inapt.

She was accustomed to their curiosity now, and able to ignore them. As she ate, however, she became aware of a very persistant scrutiny from about four tables away, where a man and woman sat together, the man facing her. For a moment she wondered if it was someone they knew, and then she decided she had never seen him before. He looked a little younger than her father, pleasant in appearance, but he simply could not keep his eyes off her, yet when their eyes met, it was he who turned away.

'Is something wrong?' Jack asked, noticing her expression.

'There's a man behind you who keeps staring.'

'Isn't there always?'

'I know. I thought we might know him but we don't.'

'Some young lout?' Jack asked, not wishing to turn and stare in turn.

'No, older. He's at it again.'

'Shall I do something about it?'

'Please don't. It's all right.'

It was another little incident which added to her determination to get out of the limelight. It was fantastic being a world champion, but what did it really mean? Nothing. She had not been born with the competitive spirit. A championship in itself brought no special satisfaction to her. It had been nice at first to think that she had done something for Britain, for she was proud of her nationality, but the feeling had passed. There were others whose whole lives were bound up in athletics, who could do just as well, she was sure. She had too many other interests. Suddenly the thought of Lenk, at the top of the Hahnenmoos Pass above Adelboden, was intensely attractive.

She would love to sleep in her own bedroom tonight, with its bright colours and its lovely view out over the broad valley below.

She sighed quietly.

Doris Ormonde, meantime, had been puzzled by her escort's sudden lapse into silence. Roy had been discussing, with much amusing comment, the autobiography of a famous man of letters. Roy at his best made good listening and Doris had been enjoying it when his attention had begun to wander. The discussion had tailed off and now he did not even seem to hear her own remarks to him. It was unlike him. She realised that he was staring past her, and had been for some time. Intrigued, she twisted suddenly in her seat and caught Janie's puzzled look before Janie dropped her eyes. Doris turned back to Roy.

'Isn't that that deaf girl, the skier? Jane Lyon isn't it?'

Roy nodded.

'She's been on television quite a lot

recently. I thought I recognised her. I wonder what she is doing in London. Do you know her, Roy?'

He surprised her by colouring. 'No,' he replied a little abruptly.

Doris nodded. She was thinking furiously. What was the connection between one of her more successful authors and this child?

'Like to tell me?' she asked mildly.

'Tell you what?' Roy asked.

'Whatever it is that's bothering you. I suppose you realise that it isn't flattering to me to have you stop talking and begin staring past me.'

'Oh God, I'm sorry. Was it that obvious?'

'It was.'

'I'm not good company tonight Doris.'

'On the contrary you were doing splendidly until five or six minutes ago. It's that Lyon girl, isn't it?'

'Yes. I'd really rather not talk about it. It's too completely stupid.'

'I don't understand. You said you

don't know her.

'That's true,' he replied ruefully. 'I was, what's the word? Captivated? I think that's it. I was captivated when I saw her a few weeks ago when she won the sportswoman award. There's something about her which comes through even on TV. I expect you've noticed it.'

Doris nodded silently.

'I'd read about her several times, and I suppose I became interested. Anyway I wrote to her and said I'd like to dedicate my text book to her.'

'That was a nice gesture.'

'It didn't get any reply,' Roy grunted.

'Does she know who you are?' Doris asked, nettled.

'Does anyone know?' he countered. 'My books sell what? Five or six thousand in hardback here and about twice that in the U.S.A. plus maybe thirty thousand in paperback. So how many people have heard of me? Believe me Doris, I've no illusions about being a working author. I saw how it works in Malvern. *Oh, it's Roy Monro the writer*, they said. But they don't know how to spell my name properly and most of them haven't read a line I've written. Authors aren't like pop singers, seen by fifty million at a time. We're strictly anonymous. The point is that it was quite a civil letter, and if she hadn't heard of me, she could at least have written to say yes or no.'

'Which book was this?'

'The latest. The one we want a new title for.'

'It's a good book. She's a lucky girl.'

'If you look at the manuscript again you'll see it isn't dedicated,' Roy replied dryly. 'As I said, she didn't reply.'

'She may receive a lot of letters.'

'Yes, I thought of that, but how many from authors wanting to dedicate books to her? Oh hell, Doris, it doesn't matter. I've never understood why people get so excited at having anything so unsubstantial as a book dedicated to them. That's why I stopped dedications five years ago. I must have been out of my mind writing to a strange girl, young enough to be my daughter.'

Doris Ormonde was one of those unusual people who know things instinctively. Something about the way he said the words 'young enough to be my daughter' and the recollection of his earlier remarks about being too old, about life having passed him by, rang a bell. She stared at him and he met her eye and coloured slightly.

'You're not infatuated are you Roy?'

He looked past her towards Janie and then back to her. 'You're too clever for me, Doris. Yes I am, like some pimply schoolboy. I remember feeling this way about Lana Turner when she first appeared in films. I was literally a schoolboy then. I never thought I'd feel it again.'

'Didn't you experience it with Gertrude?' she asked.

'Of course not. Oh, I loved Gertrude,' he told her with a scowl. 'It was real enough, but it wasn't any sort of hot flash. I didn't sleep badly, lose my powers of concentration and act like a fool. People don't.'

'Some do, some don't,' she murmured, wondering at the change in him.

'Well there you are. I expect it's like German measles. It will wear off. Meantime it's damned annoying. Of course I had no idea she would be eating here tonight. I assume that's her father. He looks my age.'

'I shouldn't worry so much about your age. Forty-five isn't the end of the line.'

'Almost forty-six.'

'Now you're quibbling.'

'Sorry. You know, every time I see her name in the *Radio Times* or *TV Times*, I get as excited as a kid going to a party. I can't wait for the day of the programme. I tell you, it's ludicrous in a grown man, one my age, one who was married for over twenty years. She's just a precocious kid hardly out of school,' he concluded in an exasperated growl.

Doris smiled. He did have it badly, and it was ridiculous, but it was rather

nice to know such things could happen
. . . so long as they didn't happen to
her.

★   ★   ★

The Hotel Alpenrose was one of the
best hotels in the area. Jack had had it
extensively redecorated and many alter-
ations had been made. It had a big
lounge and dining-room, thirty nice
bedrooms, an attractive bar, and its
own discotheque. It was popular with
visitors to Lenk. It had been home to
Janie for as long as she could
remember. The Lyons lived in a
comfortable self-contained annexe to
the hotel and had most of their meals in
the hotel dining-room. As a way of life
it suited Jack and Susan admirably, and
neither of them now wanted to return
to England. They both spoke fairly
fluent French and German, and most
of their friends were local Swiss.

Janie was walking through the reception area on her way to lunch when she

saw a familiar figure.

'Hullo Janie.'

Her face lit up as she recognised the tall, broad shouldered, fair haired young man at the desk.

'Chris! Susan didn't tell me you were coming. I'm just back from London.'

'I know. I've been following your famous career. I wondered if you'd speak to me.'

'How ridiculous. Have you just arrived?'

'Yes. Are you going in to lunch? Shall we go together?'

'Of course.'

She linked an arm through his and they went into the dining-room.

Chris Collins was Scottish. He came from some village near Aviemore and he skied beautifully. He had been coming to Lenk for holidays for several years. Originally he and his brother had skied at Aldenboden, then Chris had met her and from then on the whole family usually came to Lenk.

'Where are the others?' Janie asked as

they sat down at her usual table in a corner.

'I'm alone this trip.'

'What are you doing here this early? You're lucky there's snow.'

'I know. I really came to see you. I've only got a few days' holiday.'

'You cut it fine,' she laughed. 'I go to Zermatt next week to ski with Franz, and then I'll be home for a short time at Christmas and the New Year, and then off again, to Austria.'

'I thought you'd be busy. We'll be coming over to watch the championships this year. All of us. It's good to see you.'

'It's good to see you too,' she agreed readily. 'How are things in Scotland?'

'Fine.'

The Collins family owned a good hotel which had once done most of its business in the summer, but which now did a fantastic year-round trade thanks to the development of winter sports in the area. The two families were very friendly, and had a great deal in common. The friendship between Chris and Janie was regarded with profound satisfaction on both sides although Chris at twenty-six apparently still had not brought himself to the point of asking her to marry him.

'What's it like to be famous?' Chris asked her.

'It has its drawbacks. I'm giving up after this season.'

'You can't, not till after the Olympics.'

'I'm not interested in the Olympics.'

'Maybe not,' he laughed, 'but the British public would lynch you if they heard you say so. You're one of our few dead certainties for a gold medal.'

'It's so unfair. I did this for a lark, because Franz pushed me into it. I never expected to become a world champion.'

'That's the penalty for being so good. Are you serious about giving up?'

'Very.'

'Oh. I'm glad really.'

'Are you Chris?' Her face lit up.

'Yes. The Janie I know isn't a world champion who appears on TV almost every week.'

'Every month, you mean. Not every week. I shan't be appearing on it again for a long time. Serious training now.'

'Do you really train hard?' he asked curiously. He had not seen her for several months, although they wrote to one another regularly. 'Do you have to?'

'I used to think I wouldn't have to, but in this class of skiing, fractions of seconds are important. It's all so futile. I ski for the fun of it, not to arrive someplace a few instants before other people.'

'I'll keep your guilty secrets.'

They exchanged family news during lunch and then he went off to his room to unpack. Janie had quite a number of things to see to herself, and it was tea-time before she went to his room and knocked.

She opened the door and walked in.

'Everything all right Chris? How about coming down for tea?'

'Right you are. I shan't be a moment. Believe it or not, I had a sleep. I was tired.'

He went to the mirror and combed his thick fair hair, and she picked up a book which lay on the top of the gaily coloured bedspread. She glanced at it idly. *The Prince of Fools* she read. Then the author's name caught her eye. Roy Monro. That was the name of the man who had written that oddly stilted letter about dedicating a book to her. She remembered it because he had written as though they might know his name but none of them had ever heard of him.

'What's the book like?' she asked.

'Jolly good if you like that sort of thing. It's historical. He's a good writer. I read everything of his. Have you read it?'

'I don't read many novels. Is he well known?'

'I should think so.' Chris thought for a moment. 'He's written about twenty of these historical books and he's been on a lecture tour to America, so I suppose he's fairly well known. Why do you ask?'

'Just that I've never heard of him.'

'You wouldn't do unless there was a good library here — which there isn't.'

Janie turned the book over and there was a photograph of Roy on the back of the jacket. She stared at it, eyes wide. It was the man in the Café Royal. For a fleeting instant she was transported backwards in time. Then she looked at Chris.

'What on earth is the matter Janie? You look as though you'd seen a ghost.'

'No, no,' she said quickly putting the book down. 'I was thinking about something. What were we talking about?'

'Roy Monro.'

'The writer? Oh yes. I'd rather like to read that book when you've finished with it.'

'Take it now. I've read it once.'

'You mean you're reading it again?'

'It's one of my favourites. It's about

an officer in the 11th Hussars. It's very clever.'

'Is it a war book?'

'No.'

'Well what about you? Have you anything to read?'

'Two more books and half a dozen magazines. Here take it.'

He thrust it into her hand and she led the way to the door. Later, after tea, in her own room, she read the blurb under the photograph. It wasn't a very long one. He'd been born and brought up in London, and had lived there during the blitz in which his parents had been killed, near the end of the war, long before she herself was born. He had worked in an office and then become a full time writer when he was twenty one. He lived in the country. Some of his books had been translated into French, German, Italian and Dutch, and two had been filmed. It didn't tell her a great deal about him. She wondered why he had written to her. Why had he singled her out? Did he write to other people? Or was she the only one?

Suddenly her imagination was caught by the thought of this stranger sitting in his country house in England writing to someone whose name he probably hadn't known a few weeks earlier, asking permission to dedicate his book. It was probably a compliment. Why hadn't she replied, she wondered? She had considered it, but now she could not recall why she had done nothing. Probably laziness. At that time she had had a great many letters to write and she had quickly tired of it. It was probably easier just to push his letter aside.

She wished she had been more polite, but it was too late now. She didn't even know his address and in any case what excuse could there be for writing after all these months?

She put the book down and forgot about it.

# 3

It was nobody's fault that Roy did not go to Davos after all. There was a fire in the hotel, which was badly gutted, and the travel agency offered to find him other accommodation.

'I'll come to see you,' he told them on the telephone. 'Tomorrow.'

'Don't leave it too long sir. Bookings are difficult.'

He saw them the next day, and wasn't impressed with the alternatives they could offer.

'I tell you what,' he said, thinking that it had been rather stupid to book a holiday in Davos when he'd probably fall flat on his back first time he put skates on. 'Do you have some place small, quiet, with the amenities but *not* too busy. I'm not worried about social life. It's quietness I want. There must be skating. I don't give a hoot about what the skiing is like. I don't ski.'

The young man stared at this odd creature who was going on a winter holiday not to ski. If he wanted to skate he could go to Bristol. Why go to Switzerland? Then he remembered a name.

'There's a place called Lenk. We arranged a holiday in February for someone with your tastes sir. It's much quieter than most.'

They discussed it and Roy, who was growing weary of the details involved in his holiday, and who wished he had simply gone on a package tour and been done with it, left it to the agency to get him into a hotel. They were able to confirm his booking a few days later. He turned up at the Alpenrose several days before Christmas, approved both of the village and the hotel, had a hot bath and changed, and went down to the bar for a drink before dinner.

He was sitting with a pile of travel brochures and a tomato juice when Janie came into the bar. Their eyes met and his mouth opened in surprise. He made a slight movement, half rising. Janie hesitated and walked over to him.

'Are you Mr. Monro?'

'Yes.' He remembered she was deaf and mouthed the word clearly. She smiled.

'I didn't realise who you were in London at the Café Royal. I'd never seen you.'

'Please sit down.'

She sat. 'How did you recognise me?' he asked, puzzled.

'A friend showed me one of your books,' she laughed. 'It had your photograph on the back and I remembered the man who stared at me all during dinner. I recognised the name of course. You must have thought me very rude when I didn't answer your letter.'

'No. I was disappointed but I didn't think you rude.'

'I had so many letters. You've no idea.'

'Of course not. I should have thought of it. There were a lot?'

'Hundreds. We lost count. Some were terrible.'

'I bet they were. Would you like a drink?'

'No thank you.'

'What are you doing here?' he asked. 'I thought you were in Murren.'

She remembered then that his letter had not come direct to her. He had written to her care of Franz Bruggman in Murren.

'I live here, didn't you know?'

He shook his head. 'No. Lenk — of *course*. They *did* mention it on a TV programme, but I wasn't paying very much attention. I'd got it into my head you were at Murren.'

'Probably because they said I was trained there by Franz Bruggman.'

'I remember that bit. Your father owns a hotel doesn't he? It isn't this one, is it?'

She nodded and he laughed.

'Do you know, I didn't realise. I've had rather a lot on my mind recently. So you live right here at the Alpenrose?'

'In the annexe.'

'What a coincidence. I'm surprised you aren't busy training somewhere.'

'I came back today, for a short break. Do you ski?'

'No.'

'Then why come to Lenk?' she demanded. 'Most people come to ski. It's quite good here, you know.'

'I came to see if I can still skate. I have no interest in skiing.'

'But you skate?'

'A long long time ago. I even got a silver medal once — before you were born,' he added feeling slightly bitter.

'What made you decide to take it up again?'

'I don't know. I had rather a miserable Christmas last year and decided to go away this year. Naturally at Christmas one thinks of winter sports. I've no ambition to break my legs, so I thought I might as well go somewhere with an ice rink, and potter about each morning and watch others doing it properly.'

'That's unusual, to come for the skating. People do skate here of course. We have a nice rink. But they don't come for that purpose.'

'I was always different,' he grinned, and she thought that he looked rather nice, a gentle sort of person.

'I expect you were. It is difficult to write a book?'

He shook his head. 'Not to a writer. If it were, we would all be doing something else. I would find it very difficult to keep this hotel's accounts.'

Janie laughed. 'So do I,' she confesed. 'I help with them when I'm not mixed up in this silly championship skiing.'

'Will you have dinner with me?' he asked.

She hesitated. 'You'd better come to our table,' she said.

'I didn't mean that. I'm inviting you to be my guest.'

'I'd rather not, Mr. Monro. You see, since this world championship thing I have to be careful. If I sit at your table someone else may invite me and it will

61

be difficult to refuse. As a matter of fact my father has a sort of rule that we always eat at our own table. You can't play favourites in a hotel.'

'I'm sorry. I didn't know.'

'Of course. Why should you? You have dinner with us.'

'That's sponging,' he laughed. 'You must allow me to take you out tomorrow to sample the fare at some of the enemy camps.'

She did not reply to that, but stood up.

'I have to be going. I'll meet you here in the bar in an hour if that's all right.'

'Yes, and thank you for talking to me.'

She gave him a funny look, and turned away. He finished his drink and ordered another at the bar. Seen close-to, she was even more lovely than he had thought possible. She made him feel awkward. Suddenly he recalled a few lines of poetry from the past.

So rare, so full of grace,
her hair as gold;

I see her youth and weep
for I am old.

It might have been written to order,
he mused as he paid for his drink. He
was unaware that the barman was
looking at him with a new caution,
reserved for those few guests who were
friends of the family. Roy didn't exactly
feel like weeping but he cursed at
having been born a quarter of a century
too soon. One read, of course, of these
sprightly old gentlemen who married
young dolly birds forty years younger
than themselves, but in practice it was
almost impossible to bridge the yawn-
ing generation gap of even twenty-five
years. How stupid of him to be
mooning over this girl — for he did still
moon.

The best thing he could do was to
enjoy his holiday, go home, get on with
his job, and forget the pretty young girl
who had been the year's nine-day
wonder.

When she returned she had changed

into a red dress again. He remembered that the first time he had seen her she had worn red and it became her. She was slim and graceful. She did not have a drink. Instead they went into the dining-room to the family's corner table. Jack and Susan were already there, and Roy relaxed. He was good in company and he set out to be at his most pleasant. They liked him virtually on sight, so it was a gay meal with a good deal of quiet laughter. Afterwards Jack and Susan left them lingering over their coffee.

'What sort of life do you have here?' Roy asked her. 'I mean, apart from your skiing. What's your normal life like?'

'Very pleasant. I used to go to school here, of course.'

'Wasn't that difficult for you?'

'Not really. I was twelve when we came here, and I could lip read perfectly. Of course there was a slight language problem but I'm good at languages. I managed all right at most subjects. Then, there's always a lot doing in a hotel and we have summer visitors too, so life was never lonely for me.'

'Do you have many friends in the village?'

'Of course.' She laughed. 'I'm a village girl.'

'A boy-friend?'

She looked away at that. 'No. Not here anyway.'

'Ah, somewhere else then?'

'Not in the sense you mean, Mr. Monro.'

'During dinner we agreed that my name is Roy.'

'Roy then.'

'A pretty girl like you is certain to have admirers.' He felt self-conscious, crudely avuncular as he spoke.

'I am not thinking of getting married.'

'Sorry. What's village life like?'

'There's a lovely old café where I used to go a lot.'

'Why did you stop?'

'I haven't had so much time recently.'

'Will you show it to me?'

'You don't need anyone to show it. You can't miss it. It's called The Minerva.'

'Why don't we go there this evening?'

She frowned. There was no reason why not. It was early and she had no plans. She was afraid he'd find little to interest him in her conversation.

'If you want,' she agreed reluctantly.

'I think it would be rather nice. If you're not doing anything else.'

'No, it's all right. I'll let my parents know. I can't stay late. I am skiing in the morning early. The snow is good this year and I have to practise even when I'm on holiday.'

'I don't want to stay out late myself. Thanks Jane.'

They put on boots and coats and met by the reception desk and set out for the café which was only two hundred yards away. It was a fine moonlit night and the air was crisp and clear. He was about to speak when he remembered that she would not be able to see him.

66

There was no point in his talking. Instead she talked to him and he answered by vigorous nods.

The café was cosy, comfortable and well-lit. A number of people smiled and waved at Janie who smiled back. They found a quiet corner and ordered hot chocolate. It gave him an odd feeling, sitting here with her. It was astonishing to him that he should have chosen the hotel owned by her parents, without even realising it. Astonishing, and good fortune too.

Apart from remembering to sit facing her, it was really very easy to forget that she was deaf and of course she had a positive advantage which amused him. In a crowded noisy room she could lip read as easily as in a churchyard. Noise level made no difference to her.

'They asked me to write a book,' she remarked.

'Did you agree?'

'No.' She laughed. 'It was just a gimmick. I would like to be a translator.'

'What sort?' he asked, interested.

'Translating English books into French or German. That's easy for me.'

He nodded. It would be.

'Have you tried?'

'I don't know any publishers. Jack, my father, said he would try to find out.'

'I could write to mine about it. I daresay they'd have some useful suggestions. Shall I?'

'That would be kind.'

'I'll do it tomorrow.'

'Jack wants me to go into the hotel business. I don't mean he's twisting my arm, but he'd like it. He's thinking of selling out his interests in England and going into the tourist business here with everything he's got. We could enlarge the Alpenrose, perhaps improve it. I haven't decided.'

'You could manage couldn't you?'

'Oh yes. The three of us would run it together, and then one day it would all be mine. I'd get a good manager.'

'Or a husband,' he grinned.

'There's that. I don't know what to

do. I don't want to commit myself yet.'

'Is there someone who complicates things?' he asked, glad that she could not hear the change in his tone.

She nodded. 'There might be. If I were going to marry a local Swiss boy it would be different but I'm not sure I want to do that.'

'There's no hurry, surely? Your father can't be any older than I am.' That really hurt but he hoped he looked detached.

'Jack's only forty-six.'

'Then you've got years to play with. I should relax and enjoy myself if I were you.'

'I think that's what I always intended to do,' she laughed. 'Tell me about yourself, where you live. Aren't you married?'

'I was. We were divorced about fourteen months ago.'

'I'm sorry.'

'It's never pleasant. The trouble is that one keeps trying long after the marriage has failed and in the end it means bitterness. We should have got divorced ten years ago.'

Her face showed concern. He grinned at her. 'I think we're both happier now. I don't mind too much being on my own. It was terribly quiet and dull to start with.'

'Where do you live?'

'Near Little Malvern, in a cottage outside the town. It's a trifle primitive but I've just had it done up and it looks better now. I need to buy new curtains, cushion covers, and a decent bedspread. That will brighten it up a lot.'

'How long does it take to write a book?'

'It depends. A month usually.'

'Is that all?'

'It isn't ready for the printer in a month. It takes me a month to get the book down on paper. Then I spend a week or two going through it, correcting mistakes, untangling all the twisted sentences, tidying it up, and then I have to sit and retype the whole thing. I hate that bit.'

'So it takes what? Two months?'

'About that. Then I rest for a bit, make notes ready for the next one, and after about four weeks I'm raring to go again. I write about four or five novels a year. I only wrote three last year. They're earning a bit more money now. I didn't have to work quite so hard.'

'It sounds hard to me. How do you think of things to say?'

'I don't know,' he confessed frankly. 'I just do. I think it's either something you can do or you can't. I don't see how it can be taught. You need to be able to write passable English — that's a tool of the trade. But what makes a story-teller? Perhaps I'm a born liar,' he chuckled.

'Is it autobiographical at all?' she wanted to know.

'People always ask that. In fact it is and it isn't. It's all fantasy but you invariably put a bit of yourself into any book — express opinions that you want to air, although I often make characters say things I don't believe in myself. No author ever writes the story of his life

71

— not if he wants to sell books. You create people and they do things which you write about. Sometimes they do things you don't want them to do.'

'How can that be?' she wondered.

'Search me, but they do. Sometimes a person you've decided is a bad character turns out to be terribly nice and good. That happens.'

'I'd no idea.'

'I'm talking about myself, you realise that don't you?' he asked. 'Every writer is entirely individual. I have no idea how other people manage. I know some can plot a book in advance or give a synopsis. I couldn't do that. It's like being a painter. Each one is different, each one works his own way. No two are alike. It's lonely.'

'Yes,' she nodded.

'Your skiing is lonely too, isn't it? I mean, competition skiing,' he elaborated. 'You're on your own. Nobody can help. It must be very lonely standing on the starting line waiting to begin a downhill race.'

'It is.'

'A lot of competitive sport is lonely. Not team games perhaps, but other sports. I sometimes wish I'd been an actor. There's a comradeship on the stage. Actors are gregarious. Writers and painters are solitaries.'

'Aren't you happy?' she asked.

He stared at her for a long moment before answering.

'Sometimes I think I am the happiest person in the world,' he replied slowly. 'Sometimes I'm desperately unhappy. I don't think there's any such thing as a phlegmatic writer. Not among novelists anyway.'

She was silent, drinking her chocolate, looking around the crowded room. He watched her from the corner of his eyes. People probably thought he was her uncle. Instead he was more in love with her than ever. Perhaps it had been a mistake, scraping up an acquaintance. This was what he had wanted, but now that he had it, he wasn't so sure about it. He was going to get hurt and he didn't want that. He had been hurt enough over Gertrude. What was he, anyway? A moth fluttering round a candle? 'What are you, a man or a moth?' he asked himself with silent contempt.

'A moth?'

He realised that his lips must have framed the words and he flushed.

'Oh, just a passing thought. Nothing, really.'

'I wonder how you are going to enjoy skating tomorrow,' she said. 'I'll be skiing in the morning, keeping my hand in. If you like I'll join you in the afternoon.'

'That would be nice. If I haven't broken my arm by then.'

'A silver medallist?' she scoffed.

'That was long before you were born,' he pointed out. 'I was married two years before you were born.'

She could not hear his tone of voice but she could see his expression and she wondered at the look of pain in his eyes. He had just realised that turning back the clock wouldn't help. He had been longing to be twenty-five again, but if he were she would be a baby in a cot! There was no going back. He had always known it, but now the lesson was driven home.

★　★　★

It was mid afternoon before she was able to go to the skating rink. In the meantime she had found herself thinking about him. He intrigued her for he seemed such a pleasant man, and he was certainly clever enough — he must be — but sometimes she could sense his intense unhappiness. Why was he unhappy? According to what he had told her, he ought to be happy. Was it his wife? Did he still love her? It didn't make sense but perhaps he was putting a bold face on it. Despite all of which she somehow did not think that that expression in his eyes had anything to do with his ex-wife.

Janie had skated ever since she had

come to Lenk but it was not something she enjoyed terribly much for skating without music is not the same thing. She preferred her skiing. She looked for him and saw him in the corner of the rink, a tall, broad-shouldered figure, a bit on the bulky side for a skater. He wore black trousers, a red jumper and white open-necked shirt, and looked smart. He was doing simple figures, threes and double threes. She put on her skates and watched from a distance. He tried some loops and brackets and ended up sitting on the ice. She smiled to herself. It wasn't bad for someone who said he had been away from it for so long. He had a nice relaxed posture when he skated. She went up to him.

'Hullo,' he said, pleased. 'Did you see me fall?'

She nodded and he laughed. 'I never was any good at compulsory figures. I only got the bronze, and that was a bit of luck, I think. I failed my silver for figures.'

'Would you like to dance?' she asked.

'Can you?' he asked, surprised.

'After a fashion. I can follow you in simple dances. I know the timing.'

He nodded with admiration. 'They're playing a waltz,' he said and she nodded. They moved away from the barrier and she turned into his arms. The waltz is a schizophrenic dance. It is very easy to do badly, and incredibly difficult to do really well, with speed, elan and real grace. There is no ice dance which shows up a skater's shortcomings so easily. She realised that he must have been good, for he still skated with controlled yet relaxed shoulders and with a lovely precise swing. He was more than just a bumbling amateur. He was tapping the time lightly on the back of her hand with his left middle finger and she found it quite easy to skate with him once she had picked up the tempo. When he let go her hand she turned away from him and they glided in to the barrier.

'That was fun,' he laughed.

'You're good.'

'Don't flatter me. I know I'm not.'

'You've got style,' she insisted.

'I have wonderful calm while lying flat on my back on the ice,' he agreed. 'I enjoyed that Jane.'

'Everyone who knows me calls me Janie.'

'I'll regard that as an invitation.'

'It is,' she insisted.

'You're pretty good yourself.'

'When you've been brought up almost next door to an ice rink what can you expect? All my friends skate. The village people skate and ski from about the age of three or four. I was a very late starter.'

'I was even later then,' he laughed. 'I was sixteen when I first took lessons. I'd been bumbling around an ice rink before that for about a year, I suppose.'

'It's much more difficult in England,' she remarked. 'Shall we dance again?'

They danced another waltz and then a fourteen step, after which they went off to drink coffee together. Roy had

had quite enough for one day and knew he would feel stiff in the morning. He hadn't been getting enough exercise for years.

'I wish I could watch you skiing,' he remarked as they sat together.

'It's not much fun if you don't ski yourself. Have you never tried?'

'I've never been interested.'

'You should learn.'

'I'm far too old. Anyway I came here to enjoy myself. I don't mind a bruised bottom but I do object to spending my holiday with my leg in plaster.'

'There's a ski school.'

'Don't try to tempt me.'

'You're funny,' she laughed. 'Coming all this way to skate.'

'No, I came for a holiday. It's hard to explain. You see, years ago in London, I didn't have much money. I had a clerical job which was pretty awful and I lived in lodgings, and the only fun I had was skating. I always wished I could afford a winter sports holiday. My burning ambition was to skate at Davos or St. Moritz. I knew nothing about Switzerland but I knew these two magic names. Well, I got mixed up in other things and it's only now that I have the freedom, the time and the money. Everything in life comes too late.'

'You talk like someone bitter and cynical.'

'Sometimes I feel both. Only sometimes. Not when I'm with you. I'm merely telling you what has happened so that you will understand me.'

'But this isn't St. Moritz.'

'I *was* booked into that hotel in Davos which caught fire. They had to find me other accommodation and I changed my mind. I asked for some place quieter. The clerk remembered somebody coming here and recommended it. Here I am.'

'Why did you give up skating?' she asked.

He was thoughtful. 'I went to live in the country. I had a chance to buy a cottage very cheaply. I'd written my first book and I'd come into a small legacy. It was only eight hundred pounds. It was enough. I quit my job, bought the cottage complete with the most terrible furniture, and embarked on a career of writing. I was twenty-one. I had no time for skating, and anyway I was miles away from an ice rink. I lived near a place called Cirencester.'

'That sounds very brave.'

'It was foolhardy and I'm lucky I didn't lose my capital. My second book did unusually well and that gave me enough to keep me going for the next year or two. I got married two years after I went to Cerney Wick, and of course I was back in financial trouble again. Gertrude had money of her own but she very wisely hung on to that. I suppose it was about eight or nine years before I was really established. By that time I'd forgotten all about skating. Then I suddenly turned the corner, there was plenty of money, there was a film offer which bought us a very nice house and a new car, and suddenly, just when everything was all right with my career, it began to go wrong with my marriage. Life's funny that way. Now,' he concluded with a laugh, 'Gertrude has the house and I'm back to a cottage, but at least I don't have any money problems any more.'

She remained silent. There wasn't much she could say to him. It seemed a waste to her, but on the other hand she supposed it was a success story. He had managed to pursue an unusually difficult career and now he was an established writer.

'At least you're free,' she murmured.

'Nobody is ever free, but most of my restrictions are self-imposed. I'm glad I don't work in a factory or an office, even more glad I don't have to sell things to people. I'd hate that. I couldn't sell Rice Crispies to a starving Pakistani during a famine.'

'Do you get lots of fan letters?'

'Hardly any. People don't pester writers very much. My books get reviewed now, but you know, that makes no difference to sales at all.

None whatever. The books that have made most money are the ones which weren't reviewed. Of course, some people go after publicity. I don't. I don't like talking in public about my work. It's different talking to you, or to Doris.'

'Doris?'

'Doris Ormonde. I was with her at the Café Royal. She's my editor, and a very good friend.'

'The grey-haired woman?'

'That's right. She's a wonderful person. Anyway what I was saying was that I wouldn't like to be on television or anything like that. I did a lecture tour in the U.S.A. It was great fun but I felt an awful fool standing up before luncheon clubs, usually women's ones, talking about writing. It's just something I do. I don't understand it and I can't explain it. People like to use high-flown literary jargon and I have to remind them that I'm strictly in the entertainment business. I'm not competing with Shakespeare or Milton. I don't even read them. I never could stand literature.'

She laughed at that.

'I got such a lot of letters. Thank goodness they've stopped writing now,' she said.

'Do you know something,' he told her with a grin. 'I once wrote a letter to the *Times* about divorce — long, long ago. I was against it — which is one of the reasons why I stayed married for so long. Anyway the point is that I got about sixty letters that week — far more than I've ever had as an author. People tried to recruit me into weird groups, I was inundated with religious pamphlets and literature, and one poor woman wrote and said that once in each generation God raised up a man to do his work. It turned out she meant me. I had no idea what to do, so I just burned the lot. It was cowardly but I was bewildered. I've never written a letter to an editor since, believe me.'

They laughed together. Later they walked back to the hotel and parted in reception.

'See you this evening?' he asked.

'Have dinner with us again.'

'I can't do that. I asked you to come out with me, anyway, remember?'

'Not tonight Roy. I'll meet you here after dinner, then, for a coffee before bedtime.'

He nodded, pleased that she had not argued with him about joining them. He did not want to be a nuisance to her parents or to thrust himself into their company. He would prefer to eat alone. It was a matter of principle.

# 4

Jack Lyon found his new guest sitting in the lounge with a magazine. The Alpenrose was not a dressy place and Roy wore dark grey trousers and a black pullover with a white shirt and silk-knit tie. In this he contrived to look remarkably formal although it was comfortable and casual. Jack watched him for a moment. He wondered about the writer. He and Susan had discussed him, and his letter to Janie. He was a bit old to write to a young girl asking to dedicate a book to her. At least Jack thought so. He didn't know much about dedicating books. It seemed that in a very short space of time Roy Monro had become rather friendly with Janie.

He crossed over to him and Roy looked up.

'Good evening,' he said, standing.

'Please sit down. I came to see how you are.'

'Fine. Have a drink.'

'I'll have a bitter lemon. Are you dining with us tonight?'

Roy beckoned to the waiter, gave the order and turned back. 'No thanks. Janie did ask me but if you don't mind I don't think it's a very good idea. You have other guests.'

Jack nodded, pleased at this common-sense attitude.

'It can cause difficulties. Come and have a drink later on in the annexe where we live. Nobody will know about that.'

'You're very kind.'

'Not at all. It was a nice gesture of yours. I trust Janie has accepted.'

Roy blinked. 'I don't think so. We seem to have lost sight of the suggestion. Thanks for reminding me. The book is written.'

'Published you mean?'

'Good heavens no, not for months yet. It all takes time. It's with the publisher.'

'What's it called?'

'We had a bit of difficulty over the name. I'm calling it *Half to Rise*.'

'That sounds very cryptic.'

'It's from a quotation. 'Creates half to rise and half to fall, Great Lord of all things, yet a prey to all.' Alexander Pope's *Essay on Man*. The book is about a servant girl who makes it to the top only to find it isn't as pleasant there as she thought.'

'It sounds very deep and clever.'

'I assure you it's neither.'

'Janie told us you're divorced. Have you no children?'

'None. Perhaps as well.'

'Pardon my asking, but what made you write to Janie like that? I remember seeing the letter. We saw all the letters at that time. We had to. There were so many.'

'I know. I've been hearing all about it. I wrote because something about her captured my imagination. Perhaps it was a stupid thing to do. Why do writers dedicate their books anyway? It isn't necessary. Music and paintings aren't dedicated in the same way. In fact I'm not always sure it's the compliment it's meant to be. It was an impulse. I can be impulsive at times.'

'I see. You didn't know she lived here when you booked?'

'I didn't actually book. I left it to the travel agency and just accepted their suggestion. No, I had no idea.'

'Normally she follows the snow in the winter. She's always at home for Christmas of course and for the New Year. We used to go off together in April and do some cross country skiing. Sometimes we went in March. That's our first love.'

'It's quite different, I believe.'

'Entirely. Susan hates skiing, oddly enough. Lucky for me, for she looks after the place while I go away with Janie. Of course Janie goes away much more than I do. She really picked up all the finer points of skiing on the cross countries. You have to learn snowcraft, to judge the snow and the lie of the land. There is some wonderful downhill skiing up in the mountains but you have to be terribly good to attempt a lot of it. Of course you can just push along, and that's rather fun too. You don't have to do fancy skiing. I'm quite backward on the piste, but I enjoy ski touring and cross country skiing. It's hard exercise.'

'Half my trouble is that I only exercise my fingers,' Roy remarked.

'Janie says you skate quite well.'

'I can see she's been talking about me,' Roy grinned. 'I don't. I'm rather pleased that I didn't have to be helped round the rink, but that doesn't make me much good. I enjoy it. Janie danced with me which was rather fun.'

'You should have no shortage of dancing partners. More girls skate than men. There's always a shortage of men.'

'I daresay you're right. I haven't met anyone yet.'

'This is the time of year I like,' Jack remarked, looking round the lounge. 'Christmas and the New Year. We're busy but it's fun. Later on it is even more busy and less fun. February and March, I mean. We get pretty crowded then.'

'It must be nice to live here. What's it like in summer?'

'Beautiful. I had tuberculosis. Not badly but they advised a change of climate and I came here. I wouldn't go back now. This is my life.'

'How do you feel about all this publicity for Janie?' Roy asked.

'Between ourselves neither of us likes it, but of course we're enormously proud of her. It was a remarkable business.'

'It was,' Roy agreed. 'I don't think I've ever heard TV sports commentators so fullsome. That reminds me, I promised to write a letter tomorrow to my publishers. Janie tells me she is interested in translation work.'

'Yes, she's pretty good you know. Reading was something she naturally turned to as a child. She's tremendously fluent in written French and

German and reads a great deal. As a child she was always curled up somewhere with a book in the evenings. Of course this past couple of years she has been busier than normal — ever since she met Franz Bruggman. It's good of you to offer to help her.'

'Not at all. It's a simple enough matter. I only hope my publishers turn up with some helpful suggestions.'

'It will give her an interest which she needs. She's a bit too wrapped up in us and in the hotel. I tried to get her to go to Scotland once or twice but she doesn't like going away. We have some friends who have a hotel in the Highlands. Collins their name is. Janie and young Chris Collins have been very close for several years now.'

'I suppose you worry about her future.'

'Naturally,' Jack shrugged. 'One always does.'

Roy nodded. 'She seems pretty sensible and very capable,' he remarked.

'Thank goodness for that. I must go

now if you'll excuse me. Thanks for the bitter lemon. Come into the annexe later tonight for a nightcap.'

'I'll take you up on that.'

Roy watched Lyon walk away, a squat man of middle height wearing an expensive suit. It had not escaped him that Lyon had been probing, satisfying his curiosity about this stranger in their midst.

What would he say if he could read my mind, Roy wondered? It was quite a thought.

*　*　*

During the few days before Christmas Roy settled into a pleasant routine. He took life easily, skated every day, read a lot and explored the village. He did not have much in common with the visitors who had come to ski, and was not particularly friendly with them. He went into Adelboden to do some shopping, for the Lyons had invited him to spend Christmas Day with them and have an English Christmas lunch.

At Christmas they exchanged small gifts and Roy was made very much at home by the family. It was one of the nicest Christmasses he remembered although there was nothing very special about it, except that Janie was there. It was a quiet time, peaceful, unhurried. A new guest arrived for a week, just before Christmas, a tall, gangling man with bat-ears and long untidy hair, whose name was Maurice Maxton. Roy noticed him because of his unusual appearance, and saw him down at the skating rink twice. He went everywhere with a camera, an avid tourist. The day after Christmas he scraped up a conversation with Roy at the ice rink.

'I notice you come here quite often,' Maxton observed.

'I'm no skier. I prefer to amble about the ice in comparative safety.'

'The girl — that's Jane Lyon the champion skier isn't it?'

Roy nodded silently.

'She skates too, I notice.'

'She was brought up in this village — from twelve onwards anyway. All the locals do everything connected with winter sports.'

'Of course. Have some coffee.'

Roy hesitated. He wanted another cup. What did it matter if he had it with this visitor? He nodded.

'Thank you. I'm thirsty.'

Maxton ordered two coffees and lit a cigarette.

'You're a sort of friend of the family aren't you? I've seen you going into the annexe a couple of times.'

'Sort of.' Roy did not want to talk about it.

'Were you as surprised as everyone else when the girl won the world title?'

'I didn't know them then.'

'Didn't you? You seemed rather pally. Sorry, none of my business. Haven't I heard your name somewhere?'

'You may have. I write.'

'A journalist?' Maxton asked sharply.

'No, a novelist. You probably haven't heard of me.'

'Why do you say that?'

'Because there must be about five thousand of us in Britain and the U.S.A. who write novels more or less regularly, and I doubt if anyone could name a score of contemporary novelists without racking their brains. It leaves a hell of a gap, wouldn't you say?'

'As many as that?'

'I would estimate it around that figure. There aren't any statistics. There are about three thousand new novels published each year in England alone and they're not all written by one man believe me. There's no reason why the average person should hear of the average novelist. Only one person in ten ever buys a book and it's probably not a novel anyway.'

'I'm sure you exaggerate.'

'Suit yourself.'

Roy did not care much what Maxton believed. He was rather tired of people who either pretended they had heard his name when they hadn't, or else seemed surprised that they hadn't.

'I suppose you can have a holiday whenever you want then. No boss to ask for time off.'

'I needn't work at all,' Roy answered with mild irony. 'I can always starve if I prefer it.'

'Did I say something offensive?'

'No.' Roy felt contrite. He was prickly today for no accountable reason. 'It's just that sometimes people like me who work for themselves have *harder* task masters than people in offices who get paid regardless of how much work they do, just so long as they either put in an appearance or get a doctor's note to say they can't.'

'I suppose so. I never thought of it.'

'I don't know what you do, but I expect you get a salary cheque at the end of each month.'

'For what it's worth, yes.'

'I'm not complaining, you understand, but sometimes I think it would be nice if somebody would send me a cheque every month.'

'Here's the coffee,' Maxton commented,

not looking very pleased.

He continued to try to draw Roy out about Janie, but Roy was not to be drawn. It was not that Maxton asked anything very private, but Janie at the moment was a public figure and it wasn't his job to talk about her to strangers. During a lull he asked,

'By the way, what do you do for a living?'

'Public relations,' Maxton answered.

'Oh. Maybe I should hire you to improve my sales.'

'I'll think about it,' Maxton grinned.

He left Roy, who was waiting for Janie, and Roy forgot him. Immediately after the New Year he left. Roy was having too much fun to notice the fact. It was not until two days after Maxton went that the story broke in the press.

*Ski Champion's Romance?* a banner headline in the London *Daily Comet* asked. And a photograph of them skating together had the caption 'Wonder Girl and Admirer'. The story described Roy as an 'elderly novelist' which did not amuse him at all. However his irritation at this piece of getting-even by Maxton was a minor matter. Much more to the point was the attention it focused on Janie, and the annoyance of Jack and Susan Lyon. The story carried the by-line Charlie Smith, but they soon worked out that Charlie Smith and Maxton must be the same person. There was even a cleverly constructed 'interview' with Roy, in which some quite meaningless and innocent words were made to appear highly significant. Of course reporters descended on the village in a flock. Luckily Roy was due to leave and Janie was going back into training. She decided to go at once. Roy was apologetic on her last night as they talked in the Lyon's private sitting-room.

'It's so damned unfair,' he complained. 'Just because you take pity on me and come and skate with me for a short time each afternoon that sneaking devil has to make up one of these awful speculative stories. The trouble is that anything we say only makes the situation worse.'

'It's not your fault.'

'In a way it is. I shouldn't have monopolised you the way I've done.'

'You haven't monopolised me. We haven't met very often, except for a short time to skate. Any time you come in here, my parents are here too. This is the first time we've been alone like this.'

'I know but it's open to misinterpretation. I forgot just how public you are.'

'I don't think I like it,' she said sadly.

'Nor do I. Your father is pretty angry.'

'Not with you, Roy.'

'Janie, I like you very much, you know that, don't you?'

'Yes.' She said it quite naturally with no trace of self-consciousness.

'This means I shan't be able to see you for a long time.'

'Well I shan't be seeing anyone for a long time,' she laughed. 'Not till the championships are over.'

'I shan't write very often. It's better to be careful. You have my address in England now. I'll let you make the pace.

I'll reply to you. You'll be too busy to bother much anyway.'

'I've enjoyed reading your books so much.' He had had several sent out and she had read them. 'And you have helped me over translating.' That was true too. Doris Ormonde had put Janie in touch with a publisher in Frankfurt and matters looked promising.

'Good.'

'I'm not just going to forget you,' she insisted. 'Can't you come to the championships this year?'

'I'd rather not. I'd never get near you. Leave it till summer. Perhaps I'll come over for a holiday when all the heat is off.'

'You'll send me the book when it comes out?' She was referring to the one he was dedicating to her.

'Of course. It's going to be strange, not seeing you. Our friendship has meant a lot to me.'

'You must be very lonely,' she remarked.

He nodded, thinking of her life. It

wasn't lonely whatever else it was. She had her home, her parents, her friends, quite apart from all the publicity she now attracted.

'Couldn't you take more time off from work?' she asked. 'Meet people. Join things.'

'I've never felt the urge. Perhaps if I came to live here and work I'd find things to interest me.'

'You could do that, couldn't you?'

'I'm not sure I could afford it. Buying a house in Switzerland nowadays costs a lot of money if you're a foreigner. The Swiss Government isn't quite so anxious to make things easy for expatriates as it once was. I was only talking.'

'I don't see why. Perhaps you could live in the village here.'

'And set the papers off again?' he asked, and her face fell.

'For a moment I'd forgotten.'

'I'd better leave you now. Thanks for everything Janie.'

'Thank *you*, Roy. I don't know why you bothered with me.'

He was turning away. Now he turned back. 'Because you're young and lovely and vital and . . . everything I admire,' he concluded in an oddly low key. He flushed, turned and walked out leaving her staring after him.

He ordered a fruit juice in the bar and sought a quiet place to sit. A few minutes later Jack Lyon came and sat beside him.

'I've had another reporter on the telephone,' he sighed. 'Can I get you something stronger to drink?'

'No thanks.'

'It's not a nice thing to say about one's own daughter, but thank God Janie's leaving in the morning.'

'I know how you feel.'

'Do you?' Jack gave him a calculating look. 'You know, when I read that first report something struck me. You and Janie did see one another at least twice a day every day.'

'I've already apologised.'

'I didn't mean that,' Jack smiled. 'It's just that one doesn't think of it, but the ruddy man was telling the truth. I've never known Janie take such a liking to anyone before, apart from young Chris Collins, and that's different.'

'Of course.' Roy hid his sarcasm. He did not much like hearing Chris Collins's name.

'It's very good of you to be such a friend to her. Sometimes the friendship of an older man means a lot to a young person.'

This was turning a knife in the wound with a vengeance, even if it was quite unintentional.

'On the contrary, she took pity on me. I was lonely.'

'Well, I'll be glad when this skiing is all over and done with. She can't stay a champion for ever, and once you drop from top place they soon forget you. It's a ruthless business.'

'It has to be. It isn't deliberately cold-blooded.'

'No I suppose not,' Jack agreed. 'It's heartless just the same. Glad I only run a hotel. Of course you can keep on

104

writing till you're eighty, I presume. *You* won't be too old at twenty eight.'

Roy grinned. 'Some people might argue that I should have stopped years ago, but your point is valid. Anyway isn't Janie giving it all up?'

'If they let her. It may not be quite so easy as we thought a month or two ago. What do you do now?'

'Go home, do some work. I've got plenty to keep me busy. I'll have to put in some time in the garden this spring. It's been neglected for a year or two. The previous owner of my cottage was a very old woman.'

'Switzerland is lovely in the spring. Have you been here?'

'No.'

'Of course, how stupid of me. It's your first visit, isn't it?'

Roy nodded.

'You should come back some time.'

'But not here.'

'Eh?' Jack looked up sharply and then laughed. 'I see what you mean. Well, it's a big country.'

Roy nodded. He did not think Jack Lyon would be sorry to see the last of him, despite his politeness. As for Susan, she did not speak to him often. He sensed a faint antagonism in her which he felt he had done nothing to merit — unless she had second sight and realised that his feelings for Janie went far beyond those one would normally expect between a middle aged man and a young girl.

Jack Lyon sat and finished his drink and they talked about other things. Then he went into the annexe and found Janie and her mother drinking chocolate together.

'All packed darling?'

'Yes, except for last minute things.'

'Write as usual won't you? I'll come to see you in about three weeks.'

'Of course. Did you see Roy in the hotel?'

'Yes, we've just been chatting. Why?'

'I don't know.' Janie shrugged. 'I feel sorry for him. He came here for a quiet holiday and got involved in a scandal.'

'What about you?' her mother demanded.

'There's a slight difference. I'm the one who is headline news all the time. I can expect that sort of thing. Not Roy.'

'I don't see why you're worried about him. He's quite capable of looking after himself,' Susan retorted.

Janie frowned. 'Of course he is. I just said I was sorry his holiday was spoiled. It's the first proper holiday he's had for a long time.'

'He says.'

'What do you mean by that?' Janie asked.

'Well what do we know about him?' Susan asked. 'Almost nothing except what he has told us.'

'We know about his books. I've got six of them.'

'I'm not saying he doesn't write books. Lots of people do. There's nothing remarkable about that.'

Roy would have agreed readily, yet Janie felt irritated.

'Most people don't know how,' she said shortly.

'What's the argument about?' Jack asked, frowning.

'I don't know,' Janie told him. 'Better ask Susan. She started it.'

'That's not nice,' Susan protested. 'I didn't start an argument. I merely said that there was no need to feel sorry for Mr. Monro. He has come to no harm.'

'Nobody's arguing,' Jack said and they dropped the subject. Later however, when Janie had gone to bed, and after the bar had closed for the night, Susan spoke to her husband about Roy.

'We'll have to keep an eye on Janie. She's at an impressionable age.'

'What? She's twenty-one.'

'She's led a very sheltered life, partly because we live here in Lenk and partly because of her deafness. She isn't like other girls of twenty-one.'

Jack didn't think his daughter was like other girls at all, and he was proud of her.

'What's the matter?' he said.

'Your Mr. Monro made too much of

an impression on her. She's dazzled by the fact that he's written some books that none of us ever heard of.'

Jack opened his mouth and shut it again. He had been about to say that they hadn't heard of most people who wrote for a living, but Roy had already told them about that, so there was no point in reiterating it all. Obviously Susan was suspicious of him. He headed her off.

'We don't meet many authors. I thought it was rather decent of Monro to want to dedicate a book to her.'

'That's what I don't understand. A man that age, the same age as yourself, hasn't he got plenty of other friends? Why does he pick on a complete stranger, and a young girl at that. I don't like it much. He's not coming back here, is he?'

'I don't think that's likely. He was very annoyed about that newspaper story.'

'Annoyed or pretending to be annoyed?'

'You have got it in for him, haven't you?

Annoyed, I'd say. It seemed genuine to me.'

'The sooner Janie and Chris make their engagement official the better. It would stop this sort of scandal.'

'I agree, but is there an agreement to make it official? I understood from Janie that she had made up her mind about nothing yet.'

Susan Lyon smiled. 'Naturally she'd tell you that, but this is a subject on which I do know better than you. Of course there's an engagement. It's just that she's not quite ready to admit it even to herself.'

He put an arm round his wife's shoulder and hugged her.

'You're a clever woman. I know now why I married you. Don't worry too much about Roy Monro. We won't be seeing him again.'

'He'll probably write.'

Jack kissed her before replying. 'I expect so. It would be damned odd if he didn't. You know, you fuss too much over Janie. We both do. It's habit.

110

Because she was born deaf we have always felt that we had to make it up to her. We're worrying about nothing. She has turned out marvellously.'

Susan smiled at him and nodded.

'Let's hope it stays that way. I don't want her to get hurt. That's all, darling.'

# 5

Chris Collins's next letter to Jane was a surprise to her. He was terribly upset about the newspaper stories and wanted to know when on earth she had met Roy Monro. He even went so far as to reproach her for not having mentioned her friendship with Roy to him when he had last come to Lenk to see her for a brief visit. She wrote a letter of pacification, explaining that she had only known Roy for a short time, that he was as old as her father, and that the whole thing was a stupid press stunt.

This produced a calmer response.

'I do worry about you,' he wrote in his second letter, 'and especially about anyone taking advantage of you. You are far too nice to people. It was only when I saw this newspaper story that I realised I was jealous. We'll be over to see you win the title again, and I hope you'll come to Scotland for a holiday this time. You know how much we'd all like that — especially me.'

She smiled as she read it. Perhaps he was serious about her after all. She did not have much time to worry, for she was tremendously busy and she was too tired in the evenings to bother much about anything except a good meal and early bed. It was not a bad life, tremendously healthy and in a peculiar way satisfying. She kept meaning to write to Roy but days turned into weeks and she kept putting it off. She was certain he would understand. He was an understanding person.

And then she had her fall. It was a silly business for she wasn't even doing anything difficult. She was skiing downhill very fast when something remarkable happened. Her attention wandered and she stopped paying attention to the snow. She ran into a drift which she ought to have recognised, and she fell heavily because she was totally off guard. The result was a broken leg. Franz Bruggman, when he heard, was frantic. It put her effectively out for the year. Certain other people were the reverse of frantic, for one person's bad luck is another's good fortune.

It turned out worse than mere bad luck, however. The bone was badly set and when it was discovered it had to be rebroken and reset. Janie endured it stoically, blaming herself for skiing like a beginner in conditions when she should have been alert to the dangers inherent in new snow. She lay in bed, her right leg in traction, and finally wrote to Roy.

'It was the silliest thing, and I deserve it. Of course the faulty setting of the bone was a hundred to one chance against. I shan't ski again for a long time, and I doubt if I will ever climb back to championship class. I think you know that that doesn't trouble me much.

'I have something to keep me busy. I am translating one of your books into

German. I thought that would surprise you. It also taxes me to the limit for you don't always use simple words or uncomplicated thoughts, and it isn't easy to cope, but I am enjoying it.

'It is rather funny. There was a spate of mail at the time of the accident but I haven't had a letter in a fortnight — apart from two from Chris who is coming here soon. I don't mind of course. You know that. It is just amusing, I think. The transition from potential world champion to someone of no importance is very abrupt.

'I am sorry I didn't write before but I was skiing hard and was very tired in the evenings — perhaps that is overstating it. It was a pleasant state of exhaustion really. That has nothing to do with my careless accident. It only goes to show that even the allegedly most clever person can make mistakes.

'When is our book coming out?'

Roy, who had read about the accident and written at once, was delighted to hear from her at long last, and pleased that she was philosophical about what had happened. The only thing which sounded a jarring note was the mention of Chris Collins. The fact was that he was still completely infatuated. He had subscribed to a press cutting agency and now had a book full of cuttings and photographs of her. He had given up trying to 'cure' himself. If he was going to be an idiot he might as well enjoy it. Yet he was glad she was out of the limelight at last. He did not expect that he stood much chance with her — it was too ridiculous to think of her, so young and fresh, showing other than a passing interest in someone like himself — but it was good to know that he was not sharing her with the whole world, or that part of it which follows skiing avidly. The book had just been published at last and he sent her two copies suitably autographed.

They arrived the day before Chris Collins returned to Lenk. She opened the parcel eagerly, and handled the heavy volumes lovingly. Susan found her at it.

'Hullo what's that darling?'

'The book. Roy has just sent me two copies.'

She handed one to her mother who opened it and read the dedication. Under it Roy had written, 'To Janie with love and happy memories.' She thought that was a little fulsome but said nothing. After all it was an imposing book and her daughter's name was printed inside it. She could see Janie was thrilled to bits.

'I came to tell you that Chris and his family are arriving tomorrow.'

'Oh good. Wait till he sees this.'

'He may not be as thrilled as you are.'

'Don't be a spoilsport. Of course he shall.'

'Are you getting up this afternoon?'

'Yes please. I must practise now. I don't want to be in bed all the time when Chris is here.'

'That's more like it. Let me help you to dress.'

Janie chattered happily to her mother as she slipped into some warm clothes and then went in to sit by the window of the lounge, where she could look out at the sun and the snowclad peaks. It was a strange sensation being indoors and inactive on such a day. She was suddenly glad that next season she would be able to go skiing up among the peaks, way from the crowds on the *pistes* — and next time she'd watch where she was going. It was really rather comical, a world champion injuring herself like a novice. Nobody had put it into words in the press, for which she was grateful, but people who could ski would know. She supposed, ruefully, that her name was a bit of a joke. The only person she felt sorry for was Franz Bruggman. He had had such high hopes for her.

She was happy that day because Chris Collins was arriving on the morrow. Chris was strong, attractive, very capable — the only man she had really felt deeply drawn towards. They would be able to laugh together over her accident, and the place would be brighter with him there, although it was going to be rather miserable not to be able to ski with him. He was tremendously keen, and really quite good — better than most anyway, outside of the competitive skiers.

Next day the Collins family arrived, five of them for Chris's brother Ian had married and his wife, Jennifer, was with them. There was a joyful reunion and they met Jennifer for the first time, a dark, rather moody girl, who seemed just a little bored by it all. As soon as possible Chris and Janie went into the sun lounge by themselves and he helped her get comfortable.

'Funny to see you with a leg in plaster,' he joked. 'I thought you'd passed that stage years ago.'

'Don't you start, Chris. How do you think I feel?'

'Decidedly odd, I'd guess.'

'I do,' she laughed. 'Now, let me show you my surprise. That's it there on that table.'

'What?' he asked puzzled.

'The book of course, silly. Open it.'

He picked up Roy Monro's latest novel and glanced inside. It was not the dedication which caught his eye first, but the writing on the flyleaf. He stared for a moment, and then turned to the blurb on the inside of the jacket.

'Any good?' he asked.

'Is that all you can say? My name is inside.'

'Your name has been broadcast all over the world, written in a thousand newspapers, and you mean to tell me that this makes any difference?'

'Of course it does.'

'You're a funny creature,' he smiled, putting the book down. He had a really charming smile.

'You're just jealous,' Janie rebuked him lightly. 'You're only staying for one week, I hear.'

'Yes, I'm afraid so. We're taking over a hotel.'

'Taking over a hotel?'

'Yes, at a place called Grantown-on-Spey, about fifteen miles from Aviemore.

The people who built it got into deep water and my father's taking it over. We open at Easter but there's a lot to do. I'm going to manage it at the start — for the experience.'

'Will you like that?'

'Why not? It's a nice place and it will be interesting work. It's only for a year. We hope to have another place by then.'

'You mean you'll buy another hotel?'

'Using the existing ones for security on a bank loan, yes. My father says the thing to do is to have as many hotels as possible. There's a future in the tourist trade in our part of Scotland.'

'I don't think I'd like it if we had more than one hotel.'

'It's different here. Anyway there's only you.'

'What of it?' she asked puzzled.

'My father's got two sons to provide for.'

She said nothing. It was none of her business.

'Will you go back to competition skiing again?' he asked.

'No, definitely not. I may not even be able to.'

'Is your leg badly hurt?'

'It's going to be in plaster for quite a long time, and it may never be quite as strong as the other one again. I'm not deformed or anything — at least I hope not. I'll ski again, but competition skiing is a different matter. The standard is so fantastically high nowadays, and you've got to be a hundred percent fit. The least little thing can make all the difference. Anyway I don't want to go back to it, after a year away. I'm getting a bit old. I'd be twenty-two before I competed again, after a year away — that makes it difficult.'

'You sound like an old old woman,' he laughed.

'I was sitting at the window feeling like one yesterday.'

'Can you go out at all?'

'I'm not supposed to try to walk yet — not for a few more days. There's a sled I can sit on — Jack rigged up a chair on it. He's taken me out once or twice. Rather like a wheelchair on runners,' she added with a chuckle.

'Then shall we go out? I'm sure you get fed up with being indoors.'

'You've no idea Chris. I hate it.'

He collected some warm things and brought the sled to the side door, and then helped her into the chair which Jack had fastened to it. He dragged her along to the vicinity of one of the ski lifts and they watched for a time. It would not be light for very much longer, but Janie was glad to be out in the fresh air again. Chris stood beside her watching the skiers.

'What's the skiing like at home?' she asked him.

'Very good. I've been out quite a lot so far this year. I shan't have much time for it when I go to Grantown, worse luck. Janie, why don't you come and visit Grantown? As soon as you can travel, I mean. We'd look after you at the hotel.'

'It's going to be quite a long time before I can walk without a stick.'

'That doesn't matter. Come as soon as you can. We'll fix you up comfortably.'

'You mean, come on my own?'

'Why not?' he asked grinning. 'It's a hotel. You'll be safe.'

'I suppose so,' she smiled back. 'I hadn't thought about it, Chris. I've got some work to do. Perhaps I'll leave it till summer.'

'Summer? That's months off.'

'I'll be able to get around better by then. I *may* be in a walking plaster for six or seven months you know.'

'You've already been in plaster a month.'

'Yes but remember they discovered the leg was badly set. Leave it till summer, Chris.'

'What's this work?' he demanded, a little irritated.

'You'll never guess,' she laughed. 'I'm translating one of Roy Monro's books for a publisher in Frankfurt.'

'That author?'

'Yes, who else?'

'He must be a crafty old man. What sort of hold does he have on you?' Chris asked, keeping his tone light.

'He is not an old man.'

'Old enough to be my father.'

'Hardly. You're twenty-seven. Anyway I don't know what's got into you Chris. I wanted to do some translating, I told Roy, he wrote to his publishers and they put me on to these people in Frankfurt. It's just coincidence it's one of Roy's books.'

'They've given you a book to translate just like that?'

'Why not? If I don't do it to suit them I don't get paid.'

'Even so it takes time. I'm surprised they didn't give you something quite short to try you out.'

Janie frowned. She had not thought of that. It was true when he put it that way — they were taking a bit of a chance on her.

'I didn't think about it much. Perhaps they're trying me out. Maybe there is somebody else checking on my work.'

'There's bound to be, isn't there?' he asked.

'Yes, I suppose there is. What's so odd about that?'

'Nothing.' He shook his head and looked past her into the distance. 'You seem to be pretty friendly with Monro. Hasn't he got any friends his own age.'

'You keep talking about his age,' she protested. 'Why? He doesn't look much older than you do.'

'He may not, but he's nearly twenty years older than I am.'

'What of it, Chris?' she asked, nettled. 'Do you object to my knowing him?'

He shook his head but he did not smile. 'It's your business, not mine. I do wish you'd come to Scotland next month.'

'I'll come in July, that's a promise.'

'July! I'll be busy in July.'

'I shan't need wet nursing.'

'It's so far off. Janie I've gone about this all wrong. I probably ought not to say anything till tomorrow or the next day, now that I've spoiled it all. You see, I wanted to ask you to marry me, today. That's why I was so anxious for us to come out together, to get away from the others. I'm a fool, for I've messed it all up.'

'No you haven't.'

'You mean you agree?' he asked, looking at her eagerly.

'No Chris. Not so fast.'

'Oh, I thought . . . Well, will you marry me or won't you, Janie?'

'Can I please have time to think about it?'

'Yes. Didn't you know I'd ask?' he added, feeling curious.

'I might have guessed, but a girl doesn't like to have to guess. I decided I'd wait and see what happened.'

'Janie, I've wanted this for a long time. I almost said something the year before last. I wish now I had. Then you got mixed up with Bruggman and went into training and I thought I'd better wait. Anyway you weren't twenty-one then. I began to think I might have to wait till you were an olympic gold medalist or something. Now you've broken your leg and you want to give up, well, now I can ask you. It isn't something new.'

'Thanks Chris. You don't have to work so hard to convince me.'

'I wish you'd say yes.'

'I really do have to think about it,' she smiled.

'There's no one else is there?' he asked apprehensively and she laughed.

'How could there be?'

'You never know. I thought you might be dazzled by your literary friend.'

'Roy?' She was astonished.

'It was only a thought.'

'Honestly Chris. Why would he be interested in anyone like me?'

'Why shouldn't he?' Chris asked loyally. 'Why are we talking about him anyway?'

She gave him a twinkling smile. 'I can't think. We'd better go back.'

'When do I get my answer.'

'July.'

'Oh Janie.'

'Stop and think,' she said mildly. 'You'd want me to come and live in Scotland. Jack would rather like me to stay here in Lenk and help with the hotel, make a career of his business.'

'Couldn't we do both somehow?'

'How?' she asked and he was silent. It was unanswerable. 'You see?' she went on. 'Big decisions are involved. If it weren't for you I'd have given my father an answer a long time ago.'

'Then you do care?'

'I care a lot. The question is, do I care enough? I'm having to give up a great deal, and I'm not even sure I'd like Scotland.'

'It's wonderful.'

'So's Switzerland.'

'But they're foreigners,' he complained.

'So are you Scots,' she laughed. 'Sorry Chris, but I must think it out in my own way. If I marry you will I be able to do things — help in the hotel or do my translating, do *something* interesting and useful?'

'Of course. Whatever you want.'

'I suppose it might be possible to have some sort of merger,' she mused half to herself. 'A company with hotels in Scotland and Switzerland. Suppose we became a sort of winter sports agency for ourselves? Could anything be worked out along these lines?'

'I expect so.' He showed sudden new interest. 'What would your father say?'

'I've no idea. I must talk to him about it. It isn't a condition of our marrying or anything. I'd just like to know.'

'Do you . . . do you love me?' he asked self-consciously.

'I don't know Chris. I'm terribly fond of you. Do you love me?'

'You know I do.'

'How do I know?' You've never said so.'

'Haven't I? Well I do.'

She glanced at him, so tall and godlike, in his thick red sweater with the white roll neck shirt under it, and the tight black trousers which outlined his sturdy legs. He looked much more of an athlete than he really was. He had a good figure. It was one of his assets. He was very confident, very sure of himself as a general rule. She had always admired this positive aspect of his nature. Was it because of this that he was so undemonstrative, she wondered? It would be nice to see a bit more overt enthusiasm for her. He might even hold her hand some time.

As he started to pull the sledge back to the hotel she bit her lip. It had been a very unromantic romantic interlude.

* * *

Jack listened to her in silence as she advanced her hesitant embryonic ideas about merging the interests of the two families.

'I see what you mean darling. It could be done I suppose. I'm not absolutely certain I'd want to go into partnership with Walter Collins though.'

'Why not Jack?'

131

'Because he likes hogging things. Can you imagine him in any position except the driver's seat?'

She thought before shaking her head. 'No.'

'I think I'd prefer to paddle my own canoe, at the moment at least. Did he suggest this to you?'

'It was all my idea. I thought I'd try it out on you.'

A sudden belated thought crossed his mind. 'Is this something to do with you and Chris?'

'Not directly.'

'Chris didn't ask you, did he?'

'No,' she said promptly and truthfully. 'I'm sure it never crossed Chris's mind.'

'Chris is like his father. I can see either of them taking over other people, but not going into partnership. I like my independence here. I'm not saying it wouldn't work darling. Probably it could be turned into something quite big. It's just that I've never had any ambition to be part of something big.

I've always been independent.'

'Perhaps you're wise.'

'What made you think of it anyway?'

'Chris asked me to marry him.'

'Oh lord.' Her father's jaw dropped. 'I've botched it properly. Your mother will give me hell for this. If it's a question of you and Chris that's different.'

'No it isn't. Chris asked me and I couldn't make up my mind. I wondered about this and I wanted a straight answer and I've got it. So that's the end of that.'

'He wants you to leave Switzerland?'

'Yes.'

'We always knew it might come to that.'

'Did you?' she asked.

'Oh yes. Your mother and I have often talked about your future. Let's be frank, darling. Not all men want a deaf wife. We're used to it, and Chris loves you despite it. It can be a nuisance. You probably don't realise how frequently people speak to one another when they're out of the direct line of vision. It goes on all the time. As I say, we've adjusted. We've had lots of time.'

'You don't have to tell me. I've seen it before. People sometimes get furious if they speak and you don't answer. I imagine all deaf people suffer from that kind of thing. Chris will still have to get used to me, even if he has known us for five or six years. He's only met us on holiday.'

'If he loves you, it will be all right,' Jack told her with a friendly grin. He put an arm round her shoulder. 'He's a decent youngster and he's got good business prospects. There's money in that family. It all helps.'

'I know,' she murmured, half to herself. 'I know.'

'Is something wrong?'

'I've lived with you and Susan all my life. We've been terribly happy here in Lenk. It's all right for Chris — *I'm* going to be uprooted completely. I'm not sure. I need time to think it over.'

'Of course you do; but would my

doing some sort of business deal with Walter Collins help?'

'No, it wouldn't help my marriage. I thought it might help *you*. You wanted me to take an interest in the hotel.'

'Don't worry about me,' Jack warned her. 'I'm all right. This place will keep me happy for the next twenty-five years or more, and then if necessary I can get a manager or take a Swiss partner, and sit back in the annexe and take life easy in my dotage.'

'I can't imagine you sitting back taking things easy.'

'Wait till I'm sixty-five or seventy. Does your mother know about Chris and you?'

'Not from me.'

'You'll tell her?' he asked.

'Oh yes, but I really don't know what I'm going to decide. She'll be all for it.'

'She will,' he agreed. 'She's even more anxious than I am to see you safely married to the right sort of man.'

'Jack, what is the right sort of man?' she asked him.

'I don't know, honey. Some people look for money, or stability of character, or good looks, kindness, all sorts of things. Your mother and I don't always agree on this point. I take the view that the right sort of man is the one who makes you happy.'

'Isn't that obvious?'

'Not always. Other people may think he's no good, or unsuitable. If you love someone and you're happy, that's what counts. Believe me Janie, that's not nearly as simple as it seems unless you happen to love someone who is suitable in other ways. Your mother attaches a lot of importance to class, background, character. She's right of course, but these things by themselves won't make anyone happy. The truth is, darling, that nobody can really advise you. You have to decide for yourself.'

'You wouldn't mind if I married Chris would you?'

'Not at all.' He spoke quickly, but even as he spoke he knew that he had reservations. Vague, but they were there.

'There's no rush. I told Chris that I'd go to see him in Scotland in July. I'll give him my answer then.'

'That sounds sensible. Will you be out of plaster by then?'

'I don't think so. It won't matter though. I'll be used to my walking plaster by then.'

'Do you plan to go alone?'

'Yes, I thought so. I'd like to visit Britain properly, have perhaps six weeks' holiday ending up in Scotland with the Collinses.'

'Sensible, as I said. Your mother will be pleased.'

'And disappointed if I turn Chris down in the end?'

'Not necessarily. She'd half like to keep you to ourselves. You see darling, we feel special about you. I don't want to keep talking about your deafness, and anyway you know all about what I'm going to say, but when you were little you were doubly precious to us because you were deaf. It makes us more possessive than other parents.

We're always fighting it,' he added with a grin. 'Not that you'd notice.'

'You both spoil me.'

'Who else have we to spoil?' he asked.

She kissed him, feeling happier. Later she told her mother about Chris's proposal, and Susan, although she was careful not to urge her to accept, obviously was pleased. She was also pleased by Janie's caution in waiting till July. As she said later to Jack, it showed that Janie was not going to rush into anything and of course it would be all right in the end, but they'd all feel better because she had thought it over carefully.

Jack kissed her and said nothing.

# 6

By Easter Roy had licked Evanton Cottage into shape. It looked quite different now that it had decent furniture and furnishings in it. He had put in a lot of adjustable shelving for his enormous collection of books and had made a pleasant work-corner for himself in his little study, which had once been the sitting-room. He had a living-room, study, and two bedrooms, although the spare one had only been used once when Doris Ormonde came to visit him and stayed for the night.

He had finished another novel since coming back from Lenk, and by Easter he was taking things easily, making notes for something new, an idea for a book which had occurred to him quite recently. It was quite unlike his other work. He was in no hurry, for he had just received several thousand dollars from the U.S.A. via his London publishers.

Janie's name had dropped right out of the news. So far as things went at the moment, she might never have existed. Worse still, he had not heard from her for some weeks. There was no reason why she should write, of course. He had a snapshot of her with one leg in plaster. It was in a cheap frame on the bottom shelf of his reference book section, above his desk. That, a box containing four letters, and a scarf which he had never worn and which she had given him at Christmas, were the only personal momentoes he had of her. He treasured them.

It was incredible to him that after all the time that had passed his feeling for her had not changed at all. It was as uncomfortably acute and painful as it had been in the beginning. He had not thought that these boyish pangs could possibly last for so long. He even dreamed about her. The only person who knew anything about it was Doris

Ormonde. It was difficult to hide anything from Doris and anyway he was not sure he wanted to. There had to be someone in the world with whom you could share a little of your inner feelings.

At this point his whole life was turned upside down. A year or two before, a British film studio had taken an option on one of his early books, a story about a cavalry officer who was kicked out of his regiment during the time of the French Revolution. It had been more of an adventure story than most of his work. For some time they had been filming it, and Roy had refused to sell the rights for cash and had insisted on a small percentage of the box office receipts. It was a project he did not take very seriously. He did not know much about the film being made, but he was under the impression that it was a low-budget one. It was. What he did not know, because he knew nothing at all about cinema, was that the man who was both producing and directing it was a young genius getting his first big chance. The film became an overnight success, the book was reissued promptly, a big paperback deal was done, and within a month bookshop windows were carrying streamers about his novel. Suddenly he was news.

It was all rather bewildering. He had just begun work at last on his book about a deaf girl, and the success became an interruption. It was not entirely unwelcome. Money seemed to be pouring in at an alarming rate. Like most modern successes it generated further success. Offers were made for other books and he was fully occupied considering them, helped by Doris Ormonde who kept her head during the loud ballyhoo. He was asked to appear on TV and radio, was photographed and interviewed, and fought hard to remain casual when speaking to the interviewers. His peaceful existence was completely shattered. In addition to all this he was a local celebrity and was promptly pestered to do all sorts of things from opening a bazaar to presenting prizes at a raffle in aid of charity. Some of it he had to do, for to refuse would have given a bad impression — a bad image, he thought wryly, using the modern jargon. In the middle of it came a letter from Lenk.

'I've been reading all about you in the newspapers and magazines,' Janie wrote. 'I wonder if you will reply to me. Do you remember writing to me almost eight months ago, when I was in all the headlines? Now it is my turn. How does it feel? I hope you are making lots of money out of this. Heaven only knows when we'll see the film here, but I am coming to England in June. Can I visit you, Roy? For a week perhaps? I shall be in London of course, for a few days. Oh, I'm getting my plaster off early so I shall be without it when I arrive in England. Do say if I can visit your cottage.'

He wrote back at once.

'Of course you must visit me but you

can't stay here. I live alone. I'll book you into a local hotel, collect you each morning at breakfast time and return you at bedtime. That will take care of the proprieties. More important, when do you arrive in London? I must know your flight details so that I can come and meet you. As a matter of fact it might be fun to leave here without telling anyone where I am going. The postman and the telephone have become nightmare objects in my life. You know what it is like, so you can sympathise. I am delighted to know that you won't be lugging around a ton of plaster when you come. Do tell me all the details Janie.'

Her reply disappointed him. She did not want to be met. She explained.

'I want to explore on my own, Roy. Please try to understand. So I shall come to little Malvern on the last day of June and stay for a week, and then I shall continue with my tourist jaunt. I go on to York, Edinburgh and finally to a place called Grantown, somewhere in the Scottish Highlands. I'll send you a note before I arrive, but it will be June 30th. Could you book me into that hotel from the 30th to the 8th inclusive and I will leave on the morning of the 9th July.'

It was better than nothing. He would so much have liked to be with her during the whole of her holiday. It had not escaped him that Grantown was near Aviemore where, so far as he knew, Chris Collins's father had his hotel. She would be going to see them, naturally. It was ridiculous, but he felt quite upset with jealousy.

She arrived in the late afternoon in a chauffeur driven rented car, looking extremely cheerful and as lovely as ever.

'Did you find it easily?' he asked, as she got out.

'Yes, your directions were masterly. What a nice looking little cottage.'

'New windows and some paint helped a lot. Oh, look at your leg.'

Her right leg was quite skinny compared with the other one.

'It will soon go away. I've been out of plaster for ten days.'

'You're limping.'

'I'll tell you inside.'

'Have you been to the hotel?' he asked.

'Not yet. I came straight here.'

They unloaded her luggage and she made arrangements with the chauffeur to collect her at the end of her stay and take her up to Scotland. When he had gone she turned to Roy. 'Aren't you going to show me where you do all your work?'

He grinned and they went into the house. It did not take long to show her round and then he made some tea and they sat in his study and drank it.

'What about that limp?'

'My right leg is shorter than the other. It is quite an odd sensation. It's not much, of course, but it really affects my balance.'

'What about skiing?'

'I'll probably fall all over the place. To begin with, anyway.'

'When did you find out about your leg?'

'I forget exactly when the doctor spotted it. I haven't written to you much, recently, have I?'

'I don't mind,' he lied. 'I daresay you have other things to do.'

'I finished translating your book. They said it was all right and have sent me two others. I'm carrying them around with me and do a little work each day. Luckily there's no rush. I didn't bother to bring a typewriter.'

'Well done. What have you been doing?'

'I saw your film. I was able to follow it quite well.'

'Not mine. I only own a tiny part of it.'

'Your book then. I've been acting like a tourist in London. I've been to the Tower, Kew Gardens, the top of the Post Office Tower, the Wellington Museum in Apsley House, the British Museum, the Imperial War Museum and the National Portrait Gallery.'

'Phew. What a demon for punishment. I haven't seen half of them myself.'

'Well, now I have,' she laughed. 'I also found a really good restaurant which does Continental dishes well. It was exhausting and I shan't do it again, but I think I can truthfully say I've seen London now.'

'I thought you'd been there before.'

'Several times,' she laughed, 'but I never liked it much or paid any attention to it. Then, as you know, after London I went on a little tour stopping at Oxford and Cheltenham before coming here. I tell you, I'm a tourist.'

'I can see that,' he agreed. 'What are your plans here?'

'None. I'm in your hands. You can take me out and show me the countryside for a whole week — eight days really. I don't remember much about England. I want to see what it is like to live in.'

'I think I can keep you amused. Must it only be eight days?'

'I'm afraid so. I have to be in Grantown three days after I leave here.'

'Chris Collins?' he asked and she nodded.

'Yes Roy. A long-standing date.'

'I see. Well, tonight you eat here with me. It's something everybody should do once. I've got various places to take you on other nights.'

'That sounds interesting.' She got up. He looked up at her, at the brown, freckled face and the merry eyes, and that lovely gold hair. He swallowed hard. Sometimes it hurt just to look.

He took her to her hotel and sat in the lounge while she unpacked a few things and changed from her skirt and jumper into a dress. Then he took her back to the cottage and they sat out in his small garden, bright with flowers, and drank bitter lemon.

'It's peaceful, isn't it?'

'I found it too quiet at first,' he replied, 'but I'm used to it now. Also it isn't quite so run-down as it was.'

'It's nice. I prefer Lenk, you know, but it's nice.'

'I think I might prefer Lenk too, if it were my home. I've never really had a home, not since it got blasted in the blitz. There was my aunt, then lodgings, then my cottage at Cerney Wick, and I suppose the nearest thing to a home was the house at Painswick — the one I gave to Gertrude. I wish I had the price of it now. It's trebled or quadrupled in value. Finally there was this. That's my trouble Janie. I'm rootless. I've been alone in the world for too long. If my marriage had worked out differently . . .'

'I'm sorry Roy.'

'No need to be. I daresay a lot of people, including a great many working authors, envy me today. I've suddenly become a sort of national name. Isn't it ludicrous?'

'You deserve it.'

'If I deserve it now, I deserved it ten years ago when I'd have got much more kick out of it. I feel more like a pop idol than a writer. Still, I'm not complaining, really I'm not. You were talking about Lenk, I think.'

'I feel homesick. Is that funny? I'm not Swiss.'

'No, not funny. Natural. Lenk is home. How are your parents?'

'They're all right. They sent their love.'

'Mine to them too when you go back. I thought early supper, a walk afterwards, just along by those fields over there, and then we can catch the TV news and have something to drink before I drive you back to the hotel.'

'Sounds nice. Can I help with supper?'

'No, it's all under control. Sit here.'

'What are we having?'

'Nothing special. The sort of things I eat on my own. Perhaps a little more than usual, nicely served, but plain fare.'

He left her to enjoy the evening sun and when he called her inside the dining-room table was set in his living-room. He gave her prawns in avocado pear with a pleasant sauce he made himself; a very light and succulent mushroom omelette; cold meats with salad; and fresh strawberries with fresh farmhouse cream.

'Do you always eat like this?' she asked amused.

'Nothing here I don't make for myself but I rarely eat it all at once. That's two days' rations for me. Would you like some biscuits and cheese with the coffee?'

'Help, no. That was plenty. Let's wash up.'

'That's my job,' he told her but she would not listen to him. Instead she washed while he dried and put away the dishes, and they took their coffee outside.

'I believe that you enjoy being on your own,' she teased.

He gave her a sharp look, no longer smiling. 'Nobody does, not at my age. You're too young to know. I keep thinking of the years ahead, of doddering about here on my own when I'm seventy-five. At your age you never think of these things.'

'You don't know what I think of,' she said softly.

'No, but I know a little bit about human nature. You can't have experienced middle-aged blues yet.'

'Blues? Is it that bad?'

'It needn't be but it can be.'

'Is it for you?'

'Right now, yes.'

'Why?' she demanded.

'I don't think I can tell you the answer to that.'

'Why not, Roy?'

He hesitated. 'It concerns you,' he said shortly.

'Oh.' She frowned as she worked it out. 'I don't understand,' she admitted.

'I don't want to spoil a nice night.'

'I wish I knew what you were talking about,' she sighed.

'No you don't,' he laughed. 'Let's walk.'

They strolled silently and she was busy trying to understand him. Did her youth remind him of his own, or something like that? Was that what he was trying to say? What else could it be? They found a lane leading to a field, and leant on the wooden gate at the end of it. The air was still, the sky clear.

'Lovely,' she murmured.

He nodded. 'Very. I wish life were always like this.'

'Like what?'

'Like this moment in time, which is so perfect. You and I, the stillness, the view — everything. That's life's tragedy. It's always changing, even when it's perfect.'

'It is rather super, isn't it,' she agreed.

'Not so perfect as you, Janie.'

She looked at him fearlessly. 'What do you mean, Roy?'

'Don't you know.'

Slowly she coloured. 'I'm a bad guesser,' she said. 'Let's go back.'

'No,' he said, making up his mind. 'No, not yet. You have to know sometime. I think it might as well be now. You won't run away. I love you Janie. That's my trouble. I fell in love first time I really noticed you, on a television screen. It gets worse, not better. That's pretty odd for someone my age, isn't it?'

'I don't know what to say,' she stammered.

'I shouldn't have told you, and yet why not? Why shouldn't you know? Why ought I to hug it to myself, pretending?'

'I don't know,' was her confused answer.

'Have I upset you?'

'How?' Her eyes opened wide.

'A man my age, in love with a girl, like a moonsick adolescent.'

'It's flattering, only . . .'

'Don't tell me, I can guess. Only of course it's a one-way traffic.'

'It's a surprise anyway.'

'Honestly? You didn't guess?'

'Not for a second. I sometimes wondered why you bothered about me. You're so clever and mature — and now you're famous too. Not for running downhill, or slaloming faster than anyone else. For the things you create. It made me wonder. I didn't realise what the reason was.'

'Are you angry.'

'No, but I'd rather not talk about it,' she admitted.

'Then it's all right? I mean, we can continue with the holiday?'

'I don't know,' she told him reluctantly.

'I promise not to mention it again. It was the surroundings. That's what made me do it.'

'You don't understand. You may not want me.'

'What have you been drinking?' he asked with an awkward little laugh.

'It's rather awkward Roy.'

Intuition told him what she was trying to find a way to say. 'Chris Collins?' he asked.

She nodded. 'He's asked me to marry him. I'm on my way to Scotland to give him my answer. I'm going to marry him.'

'I see.' He felt bitterness like bile in his mouth but his face did not move. 'That's understandable. Let's just forget what's been said. Do your father and mother know?'

'They know.'

'They must be happy.'

'Yes.'

'If you're happy too, that's all that matters — even to me,' he confessed, not sure if he was being stupid. Was he really so altruistic? His thoughts were all confused.

'Thank you Roy.'

'So,' he said, becoming cheerful and businesslike, 'having played our game of confessions we can now enjoy your holiday. All right?'

'If you say so.'

'I positively insist.'

She saw that self-possessed smile on his face and did not see the agony in his eyes. He was covering up well. So she tucked her arm through his.

'All right,' she told him flippantly, 'entertain me.'

★   ★   ★

He lay awake for a long time that night, after he had driven her back to her hotel. It wasn't so much making a fool of himself; he was old enough not to let that trouble him too much. He felt spent and useless. He had dared to hope — that had been very silly. There was quarter of a century between them, twenty-five years of life and living. No girl her age wanted a man of his age. He didn't even look young, not from close-up. You could see the texture of his skin, the backs of his hands, the salt and pepper in his hair. He was presentable at ten feet, but no chicken at ten inches. Stupid man, he thought angrily.

At least he had been lucky. She had taken it in good part. He had a whole week of her company, and at that he was dead lucky. He might never see her again after this. Certainly he'd never go back to Lenk. That would be to torture himself.

It was a night of hard truth, of ruthless self-examination. He would have to get over his love for her somehow. He couldn't go on like this, mooning after her, especially now that the obvious had been stated — she was *not* interested in him. He had to think of his own future. It occurred to him that it was a damned shame Doris Ormonde was nine years older instead of nine years younger than he was. He needed someone like Doris.

He'd have to do something to make himself forget Janie. This time they had really been pressuring him over a visit to the U.S.A. He'd go for three or four months. It wouldn't cost him a thing. Financially it was a smart move. He'd telephone Doris sometime soon and tell her to fix it all up. He had missed so much of America on that last whistle-stop tour. This time he'd take it steadily, enjoy the country as it ought to be enjoyed. It was the only place left on the face of the earth where an Englishman could go and feel even remotely at home. Yes, he wanted to go to America. Maybe he ought to be smart and stay there permanently. He wondered what sort of taxes Americans paid.

His mind remained active until about four-thirty and then he dropped off into an uneasy sleep. He awoke with a headache and eyes that felt like sandpaper. He glanced at the alarm. It was already eight, and it felt like six a.m. He got up, had a very cold shower, and then shaved and dressed. He drank a cup of coffee before going to her hotel.

She looked cool, fresh, good enough to eat. All at once he wondered if he could take a week of this. One rarely had to walk hand in hand with the unobtainable. It might not be at all pleasant.

'Sleep well?' he asked.

'Wonderfully. You look tired.'

'I had a bad night. I get cramp,' he lied. He'd never had cramp in his life.

'I'm sorry. Shall we stay at home?'

'Not likely.'

He had arranged a number of excursions — to Hereford, Worcester and Gloucester, the three Cathedral cities. They explored the cathedrals and then the cities, walking up quaint alleys and side streets, looking at shops. They had lunch out. In the evenings he took her to his favourite country inns where the food was really good. The days slipped past easily and all too quickly. After doing the three cities he took her over to the Black Mountains and into Wales, north to Shropshire, then south to Monmouth and to Tintern Abbey. There were pleasant drives along quiet lanes and some beautiful scenery as she saw what Roy considered to be the best and finest part of England. There were ancient churches, fields that had been tilled for a millenium and more, and had not changed at all in that time, yew trees that had been old when the Conqueror came.

All too soon he realised with a start of surprise that it was Sunday morning, that it was her last day, that tomorrow she would be gone — presumably for ever. He dressed with a heavy heart, putting on a jumper and fawn slacks, and highly polished brown casuals. He drove slowly to the hotel and waited for her. She was later than usual this morning.

'Had breakfast?' he asked.

'I didn't want any. It's all right.'

'Shall we go home and make some?'

She hesitated. It was a dull morning and threatening rain. The good spell of weather had broken.

'Coffee would be nice. We can have it here, on my bill.'

'No, let's go to the cottage.'

They drove back and she waited in the study while he percolated the coffee in his big electric percolator. He brought it in on a tray and poured. They sat silent, not knowing what to say.

'Pity it turned out like this today. What exactly happens tomorrow?'

'The car and driver return for me after breakfast. I hope to be off by nine-thirty.'

'It must be an expensive way of travelling.'

'It is,' she agreed. 'Good job I'm not poor.'

They smiled a little wanly. Conversation was proving extremely difficult. In the end they decided just to drive for an hour or two. This time he took her east to Evesham and down to Stow-on-the-Wold and Burford. They ended up at lunchtime at a little place called Bourton-on-the-Water where they ate at a hotel. He had learned by now that silence by itself did not trouble her. One of the things about being deaf was that she did not talk for the sake of talking. When he had got used to it, he had found it a pleasant change from inane chatter. Today, however, she desperately wanted to say something but was not even sure what it was.

Instead of going straight home he made a detour to the south-west, to Painswick. He pulled up on a hill and switched off.

'What is it?' she asked.

'That's where I lived.' He pointed to a nice-looking two-storey house surrounded by a high wall. She looked back at him.

'Is that where your wife now lives?' she asked.

'Not my wife,' he smiled. 'Someone else's. She got married three weeks ago. I read about it in the newspapers. She didn't bother to tell me. I expect she'll get round to it eventually.'

'I'm sorry.' It came out almost automatically.

'No need to be. I'm glad she has found someone else. After twenty years, separation can be extremely lonely, even if the marriage wasn't terribly happy.'

'It looks like a nice house.'

'It is. You should see the inside. I went deep into debt over it.' He sighed and shrugged. 'I wonder what will happen to it, if they'll live there or if her new husband has a house of his own. I enjoyed living there, you know.'

'I should think so. It's lovely.'

'Like most nice places it's becoming crowded. Well, let's go home.'

He took the minor roads between Cheltenham and Gloucester, and returned

164

via Tewkesbury. It had been a relaxing journey and it had not rained. Somehow things went better after that. They watched television for an hour and then he showed her his cuttings book. It was an unpretentious affair started years earlier, and contained rather a sketchy collection of newspaper cuttings. He had never been famous but local authors are always natural fodder for the local press and there were even occasional press photographs. Also in the book were his school certificates and his skating certificates, and even one for life-saving dating back to his early teens. Recently the scrapbook had become fat with clippings as a result of his unexpected success.

'In a way you could call that a human lifetime,' he remarked when she had finished glancing at it. 'That's all there is to show for almost half a century of human endeavour. It isn't much, is it?'

'I think it's quite a lot.'

'Sorry Janie, I didn't say what I meant. I'm not complaining about my personal lot. I'm saying that really none of us accomplishes much. We live, we die, and we are forgotten. A handful of names live on in history books, known to a few students. It's a sobering thought. Fame really is the empty bubble they say it is. Yet we all keep trying to hang on to our individuality. It's so precious to us while we're alive, and so completely unimportant afterwards.'

'What do you mean?' she asked.

'I was thinking of a book I was reading. A few centuries ago there would be a small village on a river bank. Suppose it was Glasgow. That was a village, rather a nice one by all accounts. Everyone knew everyone else, from the most important citizen down to the village ne'er-do-well. Everybody was a person, separate, treated as such. Now it's grown. A million people live where a handful lived. It's all concrete blocks, streets, traffic jams, crowded humanity; and loneliness and emptiness. Who's an individual now? Perhaps the Lord Provost, for a year to two, or the occasional civic figure. Even the

166

biggest business man is completely un-known to half of that million — maybe more than half. We're swamped by our anonymity, face to face with our cosmic nothingness. We're ants, multiplying, breeding, dying, being replaced by other ants in an endless cycle. I think that's why religion has gone through such a lean period. More and more people are aware of the smallness and insignificance of the individual. The world may have grown smaller as a result of the growth of travel, but so have people.

'Education and travel — they're full of their own evils. The man in the village, unlettered, who had never seen the next village ten miles away, was a self-sufficient individual. He may have been miserable by our standards, but he was a person; not a digit, an ant. So we all try to retain our individuality — by wearing way-out clothing, by protest-ing, by joining groups where *within* the group we become individuals again. I saw a television programme on Vancouver, B.C. the other day, showing the high-rise flats. I think I would go completely mad if I lived for a year in one. Nothing could be more calculated to drive the irony of utter insignificance into a man's soul. Everything was so uniform — even the curtains, they said. You have to use specified curtain material and you mustn't put anything out on your balcony, or you spoil the appearance of the block. And a carpenter's son once said that the Sabbath was made for man! I wonder what he would say today. 'Stop the world, I want to get off.' A lot of people want to get off now that it's too late.'

'What are you getting at?'

'Nothing much. I was thinking how lucky we are. You were a world's champion. People wrote you letters — many of them annoying of course, but they wrote. You were a person, an individual, you stood out. Now *I'm* a bit of a best seller, for the moment. I'm having a similar experience — without so many letters, thank God. You know, everybody really wants to stand up in front of the footlights and have the audience clap. It's human to crave the applause. So few of us ever get the chance. It's not a bad analogy, the theatre. It takes a thousand out front to sustain twenty on stage. We're among the twenty — for the moment, briefly. Most of the thousand will never know what it's like. We're lucky.'

'You say strange things.'

'I'm trying to console myself,' he laughed. 'You can't have everything in this world.'

She averted her eyes, which in her case was the same as stopping her ears. He knew it and stopped speaking. Next time he saw her look up, he smiled.

'I'm sorry,' he apologised. 'It wasn't a dig at you. I hope you and Chris will be very happy. Don't lose touch Janie. You know where I live, and I know where you live. If you move or if I move, we must let one another know. That's all I'm asking — just to keep the line open.'

She nodded silently. There was nothing she could say to him.

# 7

Roy was sitting in his own car, in a side turning, the following morning when the hire car and driver arrived at the hotel. He saw her getting in with her luggage, and watched as she was driven away, out of his life. And that was the end of that. He did not feel like work, so instead he went into Worcester and spent the day wandering among the shops. He even made one of his rare visits to a cinema before going home to make his evening meal.

Janie was thoughtful on the way north to York, where they were spending the night. She didn't know what to think about him. It was flattering that someone like Roy Monro should love her. She was in no doubt about that. She had enormous respect for him, and he was the sort of man who ought to be married. He would be a kind, thoughtful husband — when he wasn't buried in his books, which was a harmless sort of vice anyway. Funnily enough she never thought of him as being her father's age — partly because her father wasn't very old anyway, and neither was Roy, and partly because there were times when she herself felt very old indeed.

Some girls, she supposed, would find it pleasant to have two men in love with them. She didn't. She didn't like complications. She really wanted to concentrate on Chris Collins and the future, for there was going to be a good future, she was sure of that. The trouble was that Roy kept intruding in her thoughts.

She considered her father's attitude. Jack was not really keen on a merger of interests with the Collins family. Instead he had decided to make the most of his own opportunities in Switzerland. Later, much later, it would all come to Janie anyway. When that happened, she and Chris could decide what to do about both the family businesses. By that time, the Collins business might be worth a great deal of money. But in his own lifetime Jack Lyon would stay as he had always been, independent.

If he felt sad that she was going to leave them, to live in another country, to become part of another family, he didn't show it. As for Susan, she thought the whole thing was expressly designed by fate to gratify her own ideas on life. Janie would be 'well' married. The word 'well' covered a lot of territory, including security and social position. The Collinses were not jumped-up newcomers. They were part of a 'good' family. Susan was sensitive to every social nuance, even after years in a Swiss village where class was almost non-existent. She had never lost her habit of labelling every visitor to the hotel. Janie realised with mild surprise that this was probably just another manifestation of Roy's theory that everyone craved their individuality in a world of increasing uniformity.

She spent the first night at York and the second at Edinburgh. She decided to stay for an extra day in the Scottish capital and so it was on the fourth day that they set off immediately after breakfast for Perth, Blair Atholl, Aviemore and finally Grantown. She saw the Collins's hotel in Aviemore, an imposing, dignified building, well sign-posted. It was only a passing glimpse but it was reassuring. It was a large hotel. The big car ate up the remaining few miles to Grantown, and deposited her at the entrance to the Royal Moray. Chris had told her in one of his enthusiastic letters about it that it was at present only a two-star hotel but would soon be a five star one. Certainly it looked nice enough, and when she looked up she saw the A.A. rating was now three stars, so Chris was obviously moving in the right direction. She smiled and went inside where she settled her arrangements with the driver of the car, and then booked in. As soon as the receptionist realised who she was, he telephoned Chris on the house phone and he came at once.

Janie marvelled at the difference in him. Here he wore a dark, expensive business suit, white shirt and some sort of college tie with stripes and shields on it. His black shoes were glossy. He had quite a different appearance from the Chris she remembered in a Swiss village, in his ski clothes or his informal *apres ski* things. He was a little bit of a stranger.

'Janie.' He kissed her cheek, held her hands and stepped back and admired her. 'Pretty as ever. Come along, I'll show you your room. The best in the hotel.'

'You shouldn't Chris.' She was not paying for this. He would not hear of it.

'Nothing but the best,' he told her.

It was a suite on the second floor front, and in the sitting-room were baskets of flowers. There was a box of her favourite chocolates on a table. Obviously the red carpet was out for her.

Chris left her to her unpacking and she did not see him again until about an hour before dinner. When he returned she was changed, and was sitting reading. 'You look nice enough to eat,' he greeted her, smiling appreciatively.

'Thank you.'

'Still reading?'

'Yes.'

'Translating?'

'I have to translate it eventually. In fact I've started. I'm just looking over the next bit, you might say.'

'Another of Monro's books?'

'No.'

'Good.' He looked pleased. 'You're not limping very badly. You said one leg was shorter.'

'It is. I try to disguise it.'

'You do it well. You look marvellous Janie. How was London?'

'London? Oh, very nice.'

'I don't know how you could stand so much of it — over two weeks.'

'I was only in London for one week, Chris.'

'I don't understand. I thought . . . '
He looked at her enquiringly trying to do time arithmetic in his head.

'I've been in Little Malvern for eight days.'

'Little Malvern? That's where Monro lives.'

'Yes, I've been with him. I was staying at a hotel but I was really visiting him.'

'For eight days?' He was amazed. 'You didn't tell me.'

'I'm telling you now,' she laughed. 'Don't look so surprised. Anyway here I am, at last.'

'At last.' He was still frowning a little. 'Have you . . . have you decided about the future?'

She nodded.

'What?' he asked bluntly.

'You aren't at all romantic, are you?'

'How can I be? I don't know what the answer is. Janie, is it all right? Are we going to get married?'

He disappointed her, but she kept smiling, that sunny, fresh smile which people liked so much, which was a sort of trademark.

'If you want, Chris.'

'Then . . . ' His face lightened. 'We're engaged.'

At long last he kissed her, and it was for the first time, on the mouth at any rate. How many girls could claim as much she wondered . . . or would wish to? She must be pretty unique nowadays.

He was murmuring in her ear, momentarily oblivious to the fact that that was one absolutely certain way of making sure she wouldn't know what he was saying, or even that he was speaking. He pushed her away and looked directly into her eyes.

'I don't know why you picked on me,' he laughed shakily. 'I'm not nearly good enough for you.'

'You'll do,' she replied with a mischievous twist to her lips.

'Wait till my mother and father hear. I'll telephone them tonight. We'll have a tremendous party, this weekend, all right?'

'All right.'

'God, I can't believe it. I've been on tenterhooks for months.'

'I'm sorry Chris. I didn't want that, but I had to be completely certain.'

'It doesn't matter now. The waiting is over.' He got up. 'Time for some champagne before dinner.'

'Not for me. Tomato juice please.'

'This is an occasion. It's different.'

'For you perhaps. I'll stick to tomato juice.'

He picked up the telephone and ordered the champagne, and some tomato juice for her, and then he sat down facing her, plainly excited.

'What about the future Janie? You'll stay in Scotland?'

'Of course. That's where my husband will be.' Saying 'my husband' made her feel a little solemn. Chris did not notice.

'And your father? What will happen to the Alpenrose?'

'Jack is going to develop it. He's selling out his other interests in Britain. He's in touch with someone in Zurich who would like to take over from him and who can help him in Lenk. The Alpenrose will be extended quite a lot. He's got a number of interesting plans, including a small shopping arcade for the hotel and one or two things like that. It would take too long to explain, but it isn't all hotel, although the hotel is the main thing.'

'He's doing this alone?'

'What he said was that when he dies it will all come to me. That shouldn't be for a very long time yet. By then you and I will know what we want to do. If we want to link up the two businesses we can do it. If not, we can do what we please. It all comes to me, but until it does he's going to stay in Lenk and run it himself. It's become his life, you see. He and Susan wouldn't be happy with any other arrangement.'

'I suppose not. Pity. I had some ideas if we'd linked up with one another. He'd have been a director.'

'He's an owner,' Janie replied in rather a cold tone, but again he did not notice. The champagne had arrived.

He poured tomato juice for her, champagne for himself, and drained his glass and poured another. He was grinning from ear to ear. There was no doubt about his happiness. They sat and talked about their future. He wanted to get married quickly, she wanted to wait till the following year in May. He was too pleased with life to put up any serious argument.

'Whatever you say my dear. You're the boss now. It seems a hell of a long time to wait.'

She noticed with astonishment that he was finishing the bottle of champagne. He poured out the last of it and sat back in his chair.

'That settles the wedding bit. May it will have to be. We're not going to be separated till then are we?'

'Of course not,' she laughed.

'You could stay here if you wished.'

'I have to go back, Chris. I shan't be seeing so much of my parents after next May. I could come over here for the skiing in the winter — say January to March? Then return to Lenk to get ready for the wedding.'

'You mean get married there?' he asked, blinking.

'Why yes. Pastor Moller will marry us. What did you think?'

'Oh . . . er . . . nothing really. Would you like more tomato juice?'

'No thanks.'

He got up and went to the telephone. As he was turned away from her she could not hear him but she hoped he wasn't going to drink another bottle of champagne. He came and sat down.

'What about between now and January?'

'Won't you be coming to Switzerland at all?'

'I don't know. I could come in November.'

'Good. That splits up the time nicely.'

'There may not be any snow.'

'I may not be able to ski very well anyway, with my right leg shorter,' she smiled.

'Oh rubbish.'

'It is not. My balance is bound to be affected. It would be funny if I became a sort of beginner again. Anyway we can always find snow *somewhere* in Switzerland in winter. It's only a question of going where it is.'

'All right.'

He sat back taking it all in until a waiter appeared with a large whisky and soda, which Chris took from him. He poured in the soda, raised his glass to Janie, and said 'Cheers.'

'You're really celebrating, aren't you?' she smiled.

'Why not? I don't suppose I'll ever get engaged again.'

'I thought you didn't drink? You never drank in Lenk.'

'I don't, not much. I have a couple in the evenings, and occasionally one at lunchtime. It rather goes with the job.'

'Oh.'

'Don't you approve?' he asked, his eyebrows drawing together.

'It isn't that. I was just remembering

what you were like before.'

'You're not objecting are you?'

She studied him for a second. There was a slight air of truculence about his expression. For once she wished she could hear his voice. She knew that for those who could hear, the voice told a lot.

'Let's not quarrel when we've just got engaged,' she suggested lightly and he smiled at her. When he smiled it was all right, and she smiled back.

'To the future,' he toasted, holding up his glass.

'To the future,' she agreed, doing the same. She sipped her remaining tomato juice while he disposed of the double whisky at one gulp.

★ ★ ★

Janie lay in bed thinking. The evening had turned out surprisingly. Chris had spoken on the telephone to his parents in Aviemore, and then they had dined together. It was a good menu, she noted; and the food, when it was served, was well prepared. The Royal Moray should succeed. She wondered how much of its present excellence was due to Chris himself and how much of it he had inherited with the hotel when his father had bought it.

During dinner he had talked about the hotel, how it was to be expanded at the end of the summer season and brought up to four or five star standard. He was obviously enthusiastic about his work in the hotel, and his face was flushed with pleasure and his eyes sparkled.

It was only later that she realised that he had been drinking steadily all night. The result was foreseeable. About eleven he had passed out quite suddenly in his chair in the bar, and the barman had arranged for him to be taken off to his room when the bar closed. It was mildly embarrassing although there was no scene as such. It was one engagement that would not be forgotten in a hurry, she thought as she lay waiting for sleep. And it would teach Chris not to drink so much. Undoubtedly he wasn't used to it.

She turned over and tried to settle and as she did so it occurred to her that the barman and the waiter who had coped with the situation had done so extremely well. It was doubtful if anyone really realised what had happened. There were only half a dozen people in the bar at the time and it was only when they had left at closing time that Chris had been taken out through a back door and spirited away.

Next morning when she awoke she lay and thought about him for several minutes. He'd have a headache today all right. She smiled to herself and then got up, did her few setting up exercises which she did every morning, and went into the bathroom where she soaked in a hot bath. He was missing during breakfast, and she went into the lounge to have her coffee, wondering what she would do today. Chris could not possibly have much free time.

When he came in he looked chastened.

'Hullo Janie.'

'Good morning.' Her smile was a welcome.

He sat down, ordered coffee, and glanced at her. 'Sorry about last night. I've no idea what happened.'

'You dropped off to sleep in your chair. That's all.'

'What on earth must you think — our engagement, too!'

'Too much champagne,' she told him. 'It could happen to anyone.'

His coffee came and he ordered a liqueur. She stared and he caught her expression and laughed.

'Hair of the dog,' he explained. 'Best thing there is. I've had a couple of aspirin. Now about this morning. I'm busy till noon. I've arranged for the hotel car and driver to take you out. Would you like to go shopping or just driving around?'

'Just driving. I don't want to see the shops yet.'

'All right. We'll meet here for lunch

and then I'll drive you to Aviemore. My father is rather tied up today so they can't come up here. We'll spend the afternoon and evening with them and drive back at bedtime. All right?'

'Fine,' she agreed.

She watched while he poured half the liqueur into his coffee and drank it off, and then repeated the process. It made her shiver just to watch it, but he looked fine.

'That's much better,' he told her. 'Now I can face the day. Janie, I really am sorry. What on earth must you have felt?'

'It was a celebration.'

'Mustn't do that on our wedding day, eh?' He winked and she coloured. He got up. 'I'm late already. Chambers will come along in a moment and take you on a tour of the district. It's lovely countryside.'

That at least was true, she decided, as the hotel car took her up to Craigellachie, down to Dufftown and back via Tom-intoul. They stopped for coffee in Dufftown.

Chambers, the driver, had given her a road map so that she could follow their progress but she preferred to look out at the mountains on either side and the rivers. By the time they had returned to Grantown she had virtually forgotten about the previous night's episode.

They had lunch at the hotel and he had changed from his suit into a blazer and grey trousers, still looking very smart and well-dressed. She had never seen him so dressy. She rather liked it. It was one of the things she had always liked about Roy Monro that he contrived never to look sloppy, no matter what he wore.

It was only a fifteen mile drive to the south to Aviemore, where Marjorie Collins was waiting for them. She too was transformed from the person Janie remembered. She and her husband had always looked smart but now she wore a very dressy dress, a lot of jewellery and a lot of make-up and it was only mid afternoon. Janie was wearing a dark green tartan skirt and a red jumper. She felt self-conscious.

'Janie darling.' Marjorie kissed her. 'Come and sit down. We're delighted. We were so thrilled when Chris telephoned yesterday evening. You look wonderful.'

Janie accepted the compliment with a little smile. She was ill at ease, just for the moment.

'Well Chris, lost your tongue?'

'No, Mother. I thought you and Janie would want to do all the talking.'

'I hope you had something special for dinner last night.'

'It was a good menu.'

'You mean the chef didn't arrange anything special?'

'No.'

'How like a man. We are having a party tonight, just the four of us.'

'Where's Ian?' Janie asked, doing some arithmetic.

'Ian and Jennifer are in Inverness on business just now. They'll be back in two or three days. We'll have a proper party then.'

'All these parties,' Janie laughed.

'Well my dear, you only get engaged once. At least, I hope you do.'

They laughed dutifully at this wit, and then Marjorie asked Chris to serve them with drinks from the sideboard. He had to ring room service for bitter lemon for Janie. He and his mother drank sherry. Then they had to discuss their plans all over again, and again when Walter Collins arrived after six. The party seemed to consist mainly of drinking, which puzzled Janie. They hadn't been like this in Lenk. People drank of course — she took that for granted. Here it seemed more of a business and less of an adjunct to relaxation.

The dinner which was served to them privately was a splendid one, six courses of which Janie was only able to eat about half. They teased her about her appetite when in fact she felt bloated. One of Roy's omelettes and salads would have been plenty, she thought, as the dinner things were cleared away and coffee and liqueurs were brought to them. She looked on with surprise as Chris accepted a long, lethal looking cigar from his father. He hadn't smoked either. Not in the past.

At last it was time to go. They said their goodbyes, promised to meet in Grantown on Saturday for a 'proper celebration' and they went out to the car. It was a cool, fresh evening. Chris led the way to his car in the car park, and Janie realised that he was not quite steady. When they were sitting in the car she touched his arm and he turned to her. He mistook her gesture and promptly kissed her. When he had finished she switched on the interior light and he frowned.

'What's wrong?' he asked.

'Are you all right?'

'Am I all right?' he repeated. 'Of course I am darling. Why?'

'I wondered if you were feeling well.'

'Never better.' He switched off the light and kissed her again. She could smell and taste the tobacco and alcohol. She found it a little offensive. Obviously it was something with which she would have to learn to live, but she hoped there wouldn't be many parties. She preferred him as she had always known him in the past.

On the way home the car showed a decided tendency to wander but he contrived to correct it safely and at last they were back at the Royal Moray. She said a quick goodnight and went upstairs by herself before he could stop her. Inside her room she leaned on the door, getting back her breath. For the first time she felt afraid. She was a long way from home and things were not what they had seemed, or at least what she had expected. All of them, Chris, his mother and his father, had become strangers. It had not occurred to her that there could be such an enormous change from them as they had been during their visits to Lenk, where after all they had stayed at the hotel and been fairly well known.

Janie was no prude. She neither smoked nor drank. Her mother and father were the same. They didn't mind what other people did. The hostel had an excellent bar. It was simply that she had come here to get engaged to a man who neither smoked nor drank, a keen out of doors sort of man, and now he did both — and certainly drank more than he ought. It was a disappointment.

She undressed; washed, and went to bed. She wondered what sort of day Roy Monro had had. At least *he* had given her no surprises, no rude shocks — apart from telling her he loved her, and that was no crime. Even if it was rather ridiculous, it was also rather sweet. Suddenly she wished she were back in Little Malvern in the hotel there, and that tomorrow morning Roy would be waiting for her downstairs, ready to take her out for the day. It had been a far happier holiday than she had realised at the time.

She bit her lip vexatiously. She was

being ridiculous. Nothing was wrong except that she was very spoiled and accustomed to getting her own way. She would have to learn to make allowances for other people, that was all.

# 8

They had gone to Boat of Garten for tea and now the car was parked by the north shore of Loch Garten. Chris took out an expensive leather cigar case, selected a cigar and lit it.

'You do this all the time now do you?' she asked.

'Not exactly darling. I smoke four or five a day. It helps with the job. Anyway you don't get cancer from cigars.'

'No.' She said it woodenly. He did smoke. It hadn't just been the celebration. Yet she had to admit that he didn't do it often. The trouble was that unlike those people who professed to like the smell of a good cigar, she hated the smell of tobacco. She had a very acute sense of smell, perhaps as people said to compensate for the loss of another sense.

'You've heard of Abernethy biscuits,'

he remarked with a grin.

'Yes.'

'That's the Abernethy Forest on our left.'

'What?'

'Honestly. Look at the map there and you'll see for yourself. They hunt the wild biscuits there during the season, which is from February 29 to February 31 each year.'

'Idiot.'

'Anyway it's the Abernethy Forest. I thought you ought to know.'

'Thank you.'

'We'll go back on the minor road, by Nethy Bridge.'

'Do you drink every day?'

'What?' He stopped, taken aback. 'What is this Janie? An inquisition?'

'No, I just asked.'

'I suppose I do, most days. Not a lot. Does it upset you?'

'I'm trying to find out what sort of person you are. I thought I knew.'

'That sounds ominous.' He smiled as he spoke but his eyes were watchful.

'It isn't meant to be. I'm trying to get to know you Chris.'

'After all this time?'

'It's the first time I've seen you anywhere but in Switzerland, on holiday.'

'I suppose it is. Can't say I see that it makes any difference. Do you think you're going to like it in Scotland?'

'It's very lovely,' she answered, thereby not answering at all. 'Didn't you say you will be leaving Grantown next year?'

'Yes, probably about Easter. We'll put a proper manager in then. I'll be going to Carrbridge.'

'Carrbridge? Why there?'

'We're opening an office. It's nicely situated between Aviemore and Grantown, and also we're acquiring a business interest in Carrbridge if all goes well. We've formed a new company. It's a pity we didn't get in on the ground floor at Aviemore, but there are lots of pickings.'

'Where were you before that, Chris?'

'We owned a couple of fairly small places in Nairn. Not very profitable, either of them. I was born there. It was only when my grandfather died that my father got the extra capital he needed. Now of course he can get money from the banks. Business is an odd affair, isn't it? It's quite true what they say — the banks only lend money to people who have money.'

'So we'll be moving to Carrbridge?'

'I'm looking for a house there. We can stay in the Aviemore hotel for a time if necessary but I hope it *won't* be necessary. It would be nice to have our own place.'

'It would.'

'My father and mother will be buying a house too. I think they've more or less got one at Craigellachie. I'm not sure how the deal is going. My father said it was a pity your father didn't come in with us. It seems we're on the brink of fantastic expansion.'

'Haven't you got enough?' she laughed.

'Nobody ever has enough,' he answered and she realised that he meant it, not in any sinister way, just as a statement of obvious fact.

That evening he was busy in the hotel so she had it to herself. She was reading quietly in the lounge after dinner when someone brought her an envelope. It was one of the receptionists.

'I'm awfully sorry Miss Lyon. This was put in the wrong pigeon hole. It came this morning.'

'It's all right. She took it. 'Please don't apologise.'

When the young man had gone she examined it. She saw the postmark and knew at once that it must be from Roy. She slit it open and took out the folded notepaper.

Dear Janie,

I found that gold butterfly brooch of yours after you had gone. You remember you took it off to show me? You must have left it on that small table in the window recess. I know it is valuable. Do you want me to send it registered to your hotel or shall I send it to Lenk to wait your return there? I could address it to your father if you'd prefer. Let me know anyway. I'm sorry I didn't spot it earlier. Shows what a lazy house-keeper I am. It was only today that I dusted in that window space.

It is very quiet now that you have gone, and I miss you. It was a good eight days and we were lucky over weather, weren't we? I was so miserable when you had gone that I spent the whole day shopping in Worcester, ate far too much lunch, and spent about thirty pounds on various things which admittedly I wanted but hadn't intended to buy just then. I have a nice pair of new string gloves for skating this winter, when I haven't even decided yet if I'll go abroad again! They've just bought another of my books to film it and I have a real problem because when the money comes in, in about a year's time, I'm going to be taxed almost out of existence. I wish I knew what to do, but I'm an absolute fool about higher finance. Isn't it nice to have money troubles caused by too much money? I can remember not so long ago when I wondered if I would ever get out of debt.

I don't know why I'm telling you all this for I'm sure you have too many other things to think about, don't you? I hope you had a nice little engagement celebration with lots of good food. I bet Chris feels the luckiest man on earth.

Guess what? My wife wrote and offered to sell back the Painswick house to me at a very reasonable price. I refused it. She will get more for it on the open market, and anyway you can't go back. You can only go forward. I'd rather stay here. I hadn't intended to write to you but I suppose I was glad of the excuse. Anyway I had to tell you about the brooch. I was in the hotel yesterday for coffee — I go there every morning now — and Hugh Alderton the manager was asking how you are. You made quite a hit with the staff although I'm not quite sure why, as I didn't think I left you there long enough for them even to get to know your name.

I hope you are very happy.

Roy.

She folded it and put it back in the envelope which she slipped into her handbag. So he was going to the hotel every morning for coffee? But she knew he never did that. He always had coffee at home at eleven. He was proud of his coffee-making. He only drank it mid-morning and after dinner, and he hated going out for it. He had said so. She realised of course what it meant. He was going to the hotel because *she* had been there She could envisage him sitting in the wooden panelled little lounge where they served the coffee. They'd had it there once, only once, while his car was having a puncture repaired. How sweet of him . . . and how sad.

Well they had celebrated the engagement all right but not in the way he meant. And there was another celebration to come. The prospect did not greatly amuse her. She was far more interested in the fact that they were going to have a house of their own. Tomorrow she was going to Carrbridge just to see what sort of place it was. Chris had been a little put out by her request for the car and driver and had said he would take her another time, but she did not want to wait. Didn't he realise how important a house would be to them? It would be their home, the basis on which their married life would rest. Men were sometimes very stupid about such matters.

It was on the Saturday morning that the letter from her father arrived, rather bulkier than usual, and she opened it and read it eagerly. Almost at once she began to frown.

Janie dear, [he wrote],

I'm enclosing a letter from Walter Collins which I don't quite understand. I thought that as you are on the spot you might take time off from your romantic interlude to ask him a few questions. This letter arrived yesterday and as you can see he seems to be very disappointed that I am not going to go into business with him. I thought that that was your own idea, and had no idea Walter Collins knew you had been thinking about it.

What I am not quite sure about is whether he expects our two interests to merge in some sort of reciprocal arrangement, or if — and this is what it looks like although he has not been specific, probably because he wrote in a hurry — if he expects me to sell out here and invest my money in him there in Scotland.

I don't want to reply to him until I know more about this extraordinary suggestion of his, but strictly between the two of us, I have no intention of doing either thing. However if I turn him down too abruptly it might offend him and he is, after all, to become your father-in-law. If business is as good as he says I can't think why he wants to let me in on it. Perhaps he is a greater philanthropist than I took him for. Maybe your engagement to Chris has softened that hard Scottish heart of his . . .

That's enough of business. I had a charming letter from Roy Monro today, in which he told me about your visit. It was good of him to find time to write when he must be fairly busy. You certainly made a great impression on him.

The rest was family gossip, and Janie turned to Walter Collins's letter. It was forceful, and the way she understood it, Walter seemed to be offering her father a share in the Collins business if he would sell out in Switzerland and put in quite a lot of money. It puzzled her, for

Walter ought to know that her father had no intention of doing anything other than carrying on by himself. She had told Chris that quite plainly.

One paragraph held her attention. In it Walter had said, 'For an investment of say two hundred thousand, or even a hundred and fifty if that is more convenient, you could look for a growth of at least four hundred per cent over ten years, which is no mean thing. Our interests are obviously connected now, and it would be good to make that connection official.'

There was a lot more of course, most of it beyond her understanding. It was true that he was not absolutely specific about whether he meant a joint Swiss-Scottish venture, or simply for Jack to put all his money into Collins. Even so, Janie like her father could not understand why Walter was making an offer at all.

Chris had boasted how the bank manager loved his father, how they were raising finance for all sorts of wonderful schemes. Why take in a partner who would automatically take a cut of the profits? Walter Collins had never struck her as altruistic. He was hard-headed — kind to his own family, but never anything except astute where money was concerned. It wasn't even as though Jack needed help. They were far from poor. Collins might have more — if he didn't now, obviously he soon would have. He was in the middle of expansion.

That didn't matter. The thing was that Jack needed no help, so why offer to make him a lot of money like this? Instinctively Janie distrusted the letter. She took her father's and Walter's letters up to her room and locked them away. She decided to see what she could find out from Walter that day when he arrived from Aviemore.

Chris found her in her room a few minutes later and kissed her tenderly. He had been more of his old self during the past two days, and she had not seen him drinking, although she could usually smell drink on his breath. She knew that in hotels it was often difficult to avoid it. Anyway he didn't drink too much, and he was less preoccupied than he had been before.

'Hullo darling. We're going to Carrbridge sometime soon. I've arranged to see over a house that will be coming up for sale at the end of the year. I'm arranging a sort of private preview. It sounds nice.'

'Oh Chris, how lovely.'

'Wait till you see it. It's a big house in its own grounds, just outside the town. Does that please you?'

'You know it does.'

'All set for a party tonight?'

'Of course. Is Ian back from Inverness?'

'They came back to Aviemore yesterday. He rang me this morning. You know, I'm the luckiest man in the world.'

She came to a sudden decision.

'Chris, tell me something.'

'What?'

'About that idea of mine about our fathers going into business together . . . '

'Yes?' He said it eagerly, suddenly alert.

'Did you ever mention it to your father?'

'Yes.' He said it slowly, cautiously.

'How did he feel about it?'

'Interested. Why?'

'I keep thinking about it. Of course you have a brother, so it isn't straight-forward, but it does seem a pity that the two families can't combine. We're both in the hotel and tourist business. You know, there are still good chances in Switzerland.'

'Switzerland?' He looked a little astonished. 'What about Scotland? This could be another Switzerland. There's a good chance to get in on the ground floor here. There is scope for a year-round tourist trade. Ian and I often talk about it. My father could be a millionaire in ten years — less in fact.'

'Honestly?'

'Of course. I'm certain *I'll* be one.' He was not boasting either. He meant it.

'I had no idea I was engaged to anyone so important.'

'I didn't say important,' he laughed. 'I said rich. We will be.'

'Then you don't really need to bother about my father. I mean, if Scotland has all that potential why should you link up with a solitary hotel in Lenk? Joke,' she added with a laugh. 'Link with Lenk.'

He made a polite face. 'Why not? Your father's is a good business.'

'It's not in that class darling. Your father must have thought me very silly suggesting such a thing. He wouldn't ever be interested in anything like the Alpenrose.'

'The Alpenrose will be in the family one day, won't it? I mean, you are your father's sole heir, and you're marrying me.'

'Yes. At least I know you aren't marrying me for money,' she joked. 'Not when you'll have too much of your own.'

She saw his expression change again.

It was clear that he had something on his mind, and that he was not ready to discuss it.

'I'm marrying you because you are beautiful and I love you.'

'There are other girls, who aren't deaf.'

'I love you.' He said it simply and she knew that he meant it. 'If you're interested, talk to my father this afternoon when he arrives. I mean, if he thinks you might persuade your father, he'd be glad.'

'Why, Chris? I can't see why?'

'Well . . . because we're all one family now, aren't we?'

'Not yet. Is that really all there is to it?'

'What else could there be?' He asked it sharply.

'I don't know. I just wondered. I don't understand business.'

'Listen Janie, I don't know if your father pays any attention to you. If the hotel is to be yours one day, he ought to. What I want to say is this. We are

going to be very rich. There's no doubt
about that. My father has plans, big
plans. We're breaking out into big
business at long last. Your father would
benefit enormously if he came to some
sort of arrangement with us.'

'What sort?' she asked innocently.

'I don't know. My father is the head
of the business. It is between them. All
I'm saying is that anyone who gets a
chance to come in with us now would
be a fool not to jump at it.'

'I see. Perhaps I'll talk to your father.
I could offer to help, couldn't I?'

'That's my girl.' He beamed at her
delightedly. 'I knew you had a shrewd
head on those lovely shoulders. Beautiful and clever. I'm a lucky man.'

He kissed her.

* * *

Once again the room was full of smoke.
Walter and his two sons were puffing on
cigars, and Jennifer smoked cigarettes.
Only Marjorie and herself didn't

smoke. Champagne was flowing, and there had been a lot of leg pulling about her not having any. Janie sat quietly, looking at the ruby engagement ring on her left hand. It was a beauty. Chris had got her exactly what she wanted. However she was wrestling with a problem.

She had managed to have a fifteen minute talk with Walter earlier in the evening, and told him that she would still like to try to get her father and him to do business together. He had obviously been briefed by Chris, for he came to the point at once.

'I'm glad you brought this up, Janie. Am I speaking clearly enough?'

She nodded.

'Good, for it's important. I have a plan which I'm trying to involve your father in. Of course I don't know if he's interested in *any* sort of plan, so he doesn't know details, but I did write to him and suggest we merge our efforts.'

'Merge them, how?' she interrupted quickly.

'Good question. I reckon that hotel

213

of his is worth about two hundred thousand if he sold it as a going concern on the open market. It may be a little less. We could soon get a valuation. What I want to do is to form a new company which would take over the Alpenrose. Your father would get shares to the value of the hotel. Simple. He'd be a director.'

'I see.' That sounded very reasonable, far more so than she had anticipated. Neither she nor Jack had thought of this. She must ask questions however.

'What sort of shareholding would that give him?'

'About a quarter. After all I've got two hotels going, a third coming up, and a tourist company being formed. I'm a bit bigger, and then there are three of us, myself, Chris and Ian. It would be roughly a four-way sharing out of capital. Your father's business would be worth approximately a quarter of the total combined business.'

'You wouldn't want him to stop work in Lenk then?'

'Good heavens no. That's the whole point. I'd want him there to run it exactly as he is doing. He could draw a salary, plus his annual dividends. He'd actually be better off than he is now.'

It sounded good. Too good. She suddenly knew it *had* to be too good. Walter Collins had overdone it. She did not know how. She had no business knowledge. She only had her intuition and it was working overtime.

'Does he know that?'

'I can't recall precisely what I wrote to him. I didn't spell it out. I'm only doing so now because I think you will try to persuade him. We want to turn this into one big family combine.'

'Would you mind if I wrote to my father and told him all this?' she asked.

'Certainly not. If you think he might seriously consider it, I'd be pleased. Your advocacy might do more than mine. I tell you what, you write first. I'll give you a little note of what I've said so that you get it right, okay? You write, and then some time in the next week or two, I'll write at greater length. If you and Chris are marrying, this seems to me to be the sensible move. I don't mind telling you, Janie, that if it were anyone else except your father I wouldn't be doing this. You see, the future is much bigger in Scotland than in Switzerland. This is where the potential is. I've got very big plans.'

'Chris has been telling me you have.'

'He's right. Not just hotels, not just winter sports. Tourism in the widest sense, and everything belonging to it. Ultimately I want to own the land, the hotels, the businesses that supply the hotels with everything from cutlery to curtains, perhaps an airline and a coach company — as much of the total operation as possible. First I have to broaden my hotel base.'

'It's going to take a lot of money.'

'Of course, but once you make a good start the banks will always advance you money.'

This was where she invariably got lost. She did not understand the role of banking in commerce and industry. So she nodded, and later he had given her a sheet of hotel notepaper with his figures roughed out on it. It certainly did look good. Jack was to get the value of the hotel in shares, at an outside valuation, plus a salary of two thousand pounds a year, and he and Susan would live free in the annexe. It was fantastic. He would have his capital, an income, a home, and a job he enjoyed, the job he was doing now. The two thousand would be pocket money. The anticipated dividends were about eight per cent, with every prospect of increasing sharply. The eight per cent was modest. Janie worked out eight per cent of two hundred thousand pounds and felt giddy.

There was only one thing wrong. Walter Collins didn't have that sort of money to give away. The Collinses lived high, wide and handsome, but she was certain they couldn't afford to be so generous. There just had to be a catch.

'What are you thinking about?' It was

Chris who had come over to sit beside her. 'You look terribly serious.'

'Do I?' She smiled at him. She guessed from watching the others that the room must be very noisy. Everyone's mouth was moving and they had that slightly strained look people got when speaking loudly.

'Yes.'

'I was admiring my ring.'

'Glad you like it.' He drew on his cigar. She saw the very faintly glazed look in his eyes. He was no worse than any of them, but it hurt her. This was no way to celebrate a happy engagement. She suspected that they would all wake up in the morning with dry throats and headaches. Even Marjorie was demolishing sherry manfully, which she preferred to the champagne of which she had drunk only a couple of glasses.

'It's stuffy in here,' she said.

'I'll open a window. It's all the smoke. I hadn't noticed it myself but you're right darling.'

He opened a window and came back to her. 'Happy?' he asked.

She nodded, a little shy. He took her hand in his. 'Tomorrow, let's get away from here for the day. Why don't we take a picnic over to Loch Ness. It isn't far by car.'

'I'd like that. We might see the monster,' she joked.

'Much more of this brandy and I'll be seeing it tonight,' he joked. 'Did you talk to my father?'

'Yes. I'll be writing home this evening.'

'Good for you. I shan't be doing anything at all this evening,' he forecast accurately.

The party went on till after ten, and then Janie pleaded a headache and they broke up. She was the only one cold sober, and she went to her room wondering why they chose to enjoy themselves in such a peculiar way. She sat at the writing table writing to her father, quite a long letter in which she not only told him what Walter had in

219

mind, but also voiced her fears that it was not as straight forward as it seemed. She sealed and stamped the envelope and then, on impulse, she pulled the paper towards her again and began to write.

Dear Roy, [she wrote],
You will be surprised to hear from me so soon after my last letter to you asking you to send the brooch to Lenk. I want you to do something for me, in the strictest confidence. I can't even tell you why I am asking you to do this favour.

Do you know any of these people (I believe they exist) who investigate companies? There is a company here in Scotland, quite recently formed, called Scotland's Panorama Ltd. I am sure of the name. It is to do with hotels and tourism. I want to find out how sound it is financially, and I would like to know quickly, but I have no idea how to go about it. I also want to know why this company

220

should offer to buy someone's hotel by having it valued, and then giving them shares in a new company to the amount of that valuation, *plus* a salary to go on managing it, and free board and lodging in the hotel. It seems a fantastic offer, with dividends expected to be about eight per cent, but it sounds like a fairy story to me.

Can you tell me how to get this information *confidentially*? And quickly?

I am sorry to write to you with such an awkward and mysterious demand. You are the only person I can think of to turn to, and I realise that you are an author not an entrepreneur, so I shall understand perfectly if you are unable to help. It is just that you know so many odd things I thought you might even know how to go about this.

I am very well. We had the engagement party tonight — just the family. It has finished now and I am going to bed. Thank you again for writing to me about the brooch. Janie.

She took it down and posted it quickly before she changed her mind. It might be very naughty of her, but she was willing to risk it. Roy surely wouldn't know the cause for her enquiry. It could be someone trying to take over the Collins hotel, just as easily as Collins trying to take over her father's. Roy knew nothing about Walter Collins and his big plans. Also the name Scotland's Panorama Ltd. would mean nothing to Roy. She would feel much happier if she could get an independent report on Walter Collins.

She had said nothing to her father about the possibility of investigating Walter. Indeed it had been a sudden afterthought. All she had done was to tell her father she felt mistrustful of Walter's motives and that she thought Walter would do nothing unless there was an advantage in it for him.

That was true, but in business people

were expected to be profit conscious. There was nothing indecent about that. It worried her that the offer to Jack should be so attractive. Jack himself would probably know how to safeguard his interests. At least she hoped so. Her father was an experienced business man. Yet he was not at all like Walter. He was quite different. If he accepted Walter's offer, and then there subsequently turned out to be some snag they had never thought of, she would feel guilty herself, because she was the one marrying Walter's son.

She went back to her room, worried. It all looked so good on the surface. She was getting worked up about nothing. There were two diametrically opposed viewpoints. From one, the Collins family were kind, generous, full of fun, admittedly a bit prone to parties but then so were millions of people, and everything in the garden looked absolutely lovely. From the other point of view, they were self-seeking cold-blooded people who belonged to a different, strange and menacing world, people who drank too much, people who were *not* what they sometimes appeared to be on the surface.

Which was right? Where was the truth? She could imagine Roy Monro's reply. She had heard him saying it once before. The truth almost invariably lies in the middle somewhere, often well buried.

It didn't help much.

# 9

Roy re-read her letter and wondered what to do. He too supposed there were methods of checking up on registered companies, official and not so official, but he had no idea how one went about it. As usual when he was in difficulty he thought at once of Doris Ormonde. Doris herself probably knew as little as he did, but Gerald Mance was a big company, a group of publishing imprints, and there must be someone in the organisation who knew something about it.

He thought it would be better to telephone since Janie seemed to be in a hurry, so he rang up Doris.

'Hullo Roy,' she greeted him. 'I'm just about to write to you.'

'Then I've saved you a stamp. What about, Doris?'

'You've passed the author's golden test.'

'What on earth is that?'

'I'll give you a clue. You and Galsworthy, among others.'

He frowned. He was no good at guessing games. 'Television?' he hazarded.

'No.' She laughed. 'Not so wide of the mark either. No, they want to publish you in Russian. Quite a decent offer. I thought you'd like to know.'

'See if you can't wangle a free pass to the Kremlin as part of the fee,' he laughed.

'Roubles, easy. Kremlin passes, not so easy. Won't you settle for being a Hero of the Soviet Union?'

'With crossed swords,' he answered solemnly. 'Seriously Doris, that's interesting news. It will look good on my blurb on the next jacket you do.'

'Don't worry, I've seen to that already. Now, what did you want?'

'Nothing so satisfactory. Doris, do you have some financial brain in your organisation who would know exactly how to check up on a development company in Scotland?'

He gave her the details and told her

exactly what he wanted.

'That's a tall one,' she answered. 'I'll speak to our chief accountant first, and then the finance director. It may take me a day or two to find out how you go about it.'

'I'd be awfully glad if you would.'

'Are you going into business?' she enquired, curious about this unusual call.

'No, it's for a friend of mine. I want to know not only if this Scotland's Panorama outfit are sound, but also why they should offer a friend of mine such an apparently wonderful bargain. There's got to be something in it for the company.'

'It sounds too wonderful for words, but I don't know how one can get to the bottom of it. It may *not* be possible.'

'I realise that Doris. My . . . er . . . friend wrote and asked me. Some people think authors are much more clever than they really are,' he added with a laugh.

'I'll try to telephone you either

tonight or tomorrow night. You'll be in after six?'

'That's right. I shan't be going out in the evenings this week — no further than the garden, anyway. As a matter of fact I'm busy for the next fortnight.'

'Working for me I hope?'

'That's right. Something different.'

'Oh lord, why do you authors always want to write something different? You do your own thing so very well.'

'This is a sort of holiday for me. I'd like to see it published.'

'What's it about?'

He hesitated. 'About a girl.'

'Are you writing romance?'

'I used to, once upon a time. I'd say more general fiction.'

'What's interesting about the girl?'

'She's deaf. Oh there's more to it than that. That doesn't make a story.'

'I'm glad you realise it. What's the rest of it?'

'Wait till you see. It's a sort of suspense thing. I think they call it a cliff hanger.'

'Oh well, that's entirely different. When do I see it?'

'Next month.'

They rang off and Roy went back to work but his heart wasn't in it at first. He kept thinking of Janie. Why did she want to know about this company? Had someone offered to buy out Collins? Hadn't she said something about *two* hotels? Yet the letter was only about one hotel. Perhaps young Chris Collins had a hotel of his own and someone was trying to take him over. If so, it was a good offer. Another thing, he thought, she hadn't sounded exactly wildly enthusiastic about her engagement. Then he realised that she might be trying to spare his feelings. After all he had told her, she was not likely to rave about her super engagement party. Yet he had a peculiar feeling that everything was not sunshine and roses. He couldn't define it and in the end he decided it was just imagination.

The following evening Doris rang back.

'About that business enquiry Roy,' she told him when they had exchanged greetings. 'There's nobody here who can help much, but we publish Laurie Lane. You must have heard of him.'

Roy knew the name vaguely. Mance's published a great variety of books and were very strong on non-fiction including university textbooks, and also a lot of excellent biography. Laurie Lane was one of their writers whose name had caught his attention.

'The chap who does various exposés?'

'That's right. We've just published *Below The Surface* and it is selling like hot cakes. Our chairman positively purrs when Laurie's name comes up. I've spoken to him today. He knows exactly how to find out what you want and he's prepared to do it for you. If it's important, I'd be inclined to recommend him. He's really a journalist, or perhaps investigator would be a better word. That's the snag.'

'Snag?' Roy asked.

'Roy dear, Laurie Lane works strictly

for money. He's prepared to do you a favour. I told him you were one of our best selling writers and he'd heard your name. For an autographed set of your books plus fifty pounds, he'll dig out all the information you want.'

'If you have his number ring him back and ask him how soon he can do it. He has a deal. Are you serious about autographed books?'

'Quite serious.' She laughed. 'People are funny. Normally he'd charge about £150 for a confidential report on a company, or so he tells me, and he says that his reports are very confidential and very comprehensive. Why don't you telephone him yourself? He lives not very far away from you, just outside Ross-on-Wye.'

'Does he? I thought of him as a city gent.'

'Oh no. He is what is known as a gentleman farmer. Money is a sort of hobby of his. He likes to study how people are motivated by money.'

'A farmer?'

'I don't suppose he's ever milked a cow. He pays other people to do it. Anyway he's at home at the moment, and will be until morning. I'll give you his number.'

She did so and Roy noted it down. When they had hung up he dialled Lane's house and Lane answered the telephone. Roy introduced himself.

After a short discussion he said, 'Well it's a deal. I will post the cheque to you tomorrow and Doris is sending me a new set of books which I will inscribe and send on. The point is, how soon can you find out for me?'

'It will take three days. I can't possibly do it in less. You realise that I've never heard of Scotland's Panorama until now. My business is knowing how to get information. I don't carry it all around in my head.'

'I understand.'

'There's just one other thing Mr. Monro. If you ask me to go ahead with this you can't call me off.'

'What?'

'Sorry to sound like a cardboard detective, but it's a fact. If I find anything interesting, interesting to me, that is, about Scotland's Panorama, then not only will you get your report but I may very well go on investigating them, and the result is not entirely pleasant sometimes. It depends on the company. So if you'd rather I kept my nose out of it, say so now.'

'What you're saying is that if you uncover anything unsavoury about this company, then you might write some sort of exposé on them for the press?'

'I might very well. I get paid a lot of money for exposing shady business firms.'

'I don't mind. I've no personal interest in this lot. It's a friend who has been approached by them.'

'Can you tell me anything about the friend?'

'I'm sorry, I can't. It is all extremely confidential.'

'Let me know your number. I'll call you back before the week-end.'

'Thank you very much.'

'You aren't too far away. I tell you what, why don't you come here at the week-end. Come on Saturday morning. I've got rather a nice house, well worth a visit. Come for lunch and bring the books and cheque with you, and I'll have your report ready.'

Roy hesitated. 'All right,' he agreed. 'I should be free by then.'

'You're working on a book?'

'Yes.'

'Then I won't disturb you any longer. Nice to have spoken to you Mr. Monro.'

Roy was fairly pleased with progress. It would never have occurred to him to contact anyone so high powered as Laurie Lane, even if he had thought about him, which he wouldn't have done. He was fairly certain that he would get the best possible advice. He decided to send an interim report to Janie.

It was quite short and in it he told her that he had found out how to get the facts she wanted, and that he would have them on Saturday. He would write on Saturday night with as complete a report as was obtainable. He didn't elaborate, for there was no basis for it. Indeed the letter was almost impersonal. He thought she would prefer it to be that way. If there was one thing more offensive than an old fool, it was a maudlin love-sick old fool. He liked her far too much, loved her far too much in fact, to subject her to that.

The two big parcels of books arrived on the Thursday afternoon and he unpacked them and sat down and wrote little personal messages inside to Laurie Lane, and signed them. For the life of him he could not see what anyone like Lane wanted with autographed novels. To some people it might mean something, but not to a man whose own four or five books were world best-sellers. Of course they weren't fiction. Was he one of those who thought there was a mystique about writing fiction? If so, it was well hidden under the sheer drudgery. In the old days men sat round the camp fire with their horns of ale, and the tribal story-teller, warm, replete, full of ale, spun his yarns. That might have been fun. Now you got up early and attacked a noisy typewriter, day after day, until one day you realised that it was finished, and wondered once again why you hadn't elected to become a swineherd or an astrologer, or anything other than a mechanised bard.

On the Saturday he set off early for Ross, and found Lane's big house, standing in several acres of lawns and parkland, about a mile to the south-east. There was a gleaming Rolls-Royce in two shades of grey standing by the arched front entrance. Roy parked his own Austin behind the Rolls and got out and unloaded a large cardboard carton containing all the books. Lane came to the door.

'Hullo. Monro is it?'

'That's right.'

'Welcome. Laurie Lane. Let me help you.'

'You might as well have asked for bricks as books,' Roy laughed. 'They weigh a ton.'

'Ah,' Lane looked pleased. He wore riding breeches, gleaming boots, and an expensive tweed hacking jacket. 'Glad you got them in time.'

He relieved Roy of the burden, picking up the box easily and carrying it in. Subdued by this display of physical power, Roy followed. Quite a man, Laurie Lane.

Once in the library Lane offered him a drink which he refused. They sat down by french windows opening out on to a lovely piece of lawn with a bird table and a sundial.

'I got the information you needed and very interesting too. I don't think I'm especially interested in Scotland's Panorama yet, but I shall keep an eye on them.'

'Oh?'

'Yes. They may get away with what they're doing. Now, you're sure of your information are you?'

'I beg your pardon?' Roy was puzzled. Lane, surely, was the one with information?

'You said that Scotland's Panorama were offering to take over a hotel somewhere, at outside valuation to be paid in shares in a new company, plus salary, expenses accommodation and so on?'

'Yes, so I'm told. It was the person involved who wrote to me.'

'Where is the hotel?'

Roy hesitated. He didn't know the answer to that. He assumed that it might be in Aviemore.

'Is it in this country? I have a reason for asking.'

'Yes. That is . . . ' He stopped as a new thought entered his mind. Was Chris Collins's father doing a deal with Jack Lyon? That was something he hadn't considered. 'Well, it could be in Switzerland, I suppose. I didn't ask. Either in Scotland or Switzerland.'

'Ah, that sounds more likely. There would be tax advantages involved. Look

Mr. Monro, how much do you know about business.'

'The name is Roy and the answer is nothing.'

Lane laughed. 'At least you admit it, which is refreshing. You'd be surprised how many people tell me all about it. It's such a waste of time. All right. It works this way sometimes. Suppose you own a hotel. We might as well make it a hotel, because that's what we're discussing. You have one that is doing well. What can you do now? The answer is to buy another. For that you need a lot of money. Perhaps eighty thousand, a hundred and twenty thousand, maybe a lot more. More than you have in the bank. You don't have any money in the bank at all, other than your operating float. Your money is all tied up in the existing business.'

'Yes, I see that.'

'So you have a chance to buy hotel B, which is good, capable of expansion and improvement, and you want another hundred and fifty thousand. You go to your bank manager, tell him all about it, and offer hotel A as the security.'

'Yes,' Roy said. That made sense.

'But you are ambitious. You don't want two hotels. You want more. You get options on two or three more. By now you need something like quarter, perhaps half a million. You need both to buy and to develop. So every property is used to secure another one. If we take this to a logical conclusion, and we are dealing with a man who is expanding quickly — too quickly — we end up with a company worth perhaps three hundred thousand and capital of perhaps ten or twenty thousand, and the rest in property which is mort-gaged. After ten or fifteen years all the mortgages are paid off, and overnight you're a very rich man. Meantime you *live* like a rich man, but if anyone called in your debts you'd be wiped out in less than it takes to say the words.'

'I see.'

'That's how a lot of business works. Now your friends in Scotland's Panorama are doing that. They've got hardly any money at all. The man who owns it — do you know him?'

'Collins?' Roy asked, guessing.

'That's right.' Lane gave him a shrewd stare. 'Collins has plenty to spend. He's not stuck for two thousand or three thousand. He has a hotel in Aviemore which is now paid for. He has used it to buy one in Grantown which is not paid for at all. The bank owns it. The bank has also agreed to advance him forty thousand for improvements. He's got an option on a third hotel, and he's formed *three* companies, for reasons which at the moment are nebulous. Now I'd say from my report that Mr. Collins is a clever man who has seen the possibilities and is determined to get in on, or close to, the ground floor. His trouble is lack of money. All right, he's got a start. Until six months ago he was doing very well thank you. Now he's in hock up to his ears. Yet he is still wheeling and dealing. He will either end up a very rich man, or a bankrupt. I'm glad to say that at the moment he is playing with his own money and the bank's. If he tries to borrow money from other people then I become interested, for right now he is a very bad risk.'

'I see. He could succeed?'

'He may be a brilliant man about to make the coup of a lifetime. On the other hand he is walking on the edge of a precipice. I don't think the outcome is entirely in his hands. Now about your friend. What was the offer?'

'To buy a hotel at valuation. Probably worth two hundred thousand pounds. It would be paid for in shares in a new company to be formed, which would be a merger between Collins and the other hotel owner.'

'I get it. That's what I wanted to check on. I'll explain that. Your friend gets a lot of shares valued nominally at say two hundred thousand pounds. Now shares are only valued at the paper they are printed on *plus* whatever the company is worth. A million shares in a bankrupt company is a liability. Ten shares in a booming one is good business. All right?'

'Yes,' Roy agreed.

'So in effect your friend parts with a hotel, which I assume he owns outright, and gets bits of paper, plus a two thousand a year job which will last only as long as the hotel lasts, and accommodation, etc. But the hotel is no longer his. He's only a shareholder, and an employee. He may be a director too, but that's neither here nor there. He's sold his business for paper promises.'

'What would Collins get out of it?' Roy demanded. 'I mean, it's a very good hotel, if it is the Swiss one. I can't be sure about that, but the more I think of it, the more I'm inclined to believe that's what it is. It's a good hotel, making its owner a very nice income.'

'I wish I owned a Swiss hotel. So what does Collins get? He gets property. He can now go to the bank and raise *another* two hundred thousand pounds. Your friend wouldn't even have to know about that. The hotel could be mortgaged to the hilt, plus everything in it!'

'Oh.'

'Now do you see? In exchange for bits of paper he gets a property to mortgage — either to provide money to stave off creditors, or else, if he is coping with that, then to buy something else. Collins thinks very big — too big for one who hasn't made very much money yet. He won't turn the corner and be safe for at least ten years. For the next ten years he's a gambler. That's how it works.'

'So my friend could lose his hotel?'

'I don't know details of the agreement of course, but I'd say he could lose it at any time. Once a deal of that sort had been made, Collins could actually sell the hotel. He won't of course. He'll get a bank mortgage, and maybe a second mortgage. If it comes off, if it succeeds, then your friend really will be well off. He'll have a lot of shares in a very prosperous company. It could double or treble his capital — in the long run. His shares could rocket. He could sell out for a fortune. It *could* happen, in several years time from now.'

'But Collins is doing him no favour.'

'In the short term? No, it's the other way round. Collins *is* in a cash bind. That is really confidential. He's been a bit too quick and he has to get some money from somewhere quite soon or he may trip up even before he gets started.'

'I think I understand. I don't know how far your advice goes, but let me tell you something. I shall tell my friend to have nothing to do with it. Do you disapprove?'

Laurie Lane grinned. 'No. I'm not going to tell him, but *you* can. I agree with you, but I won't put it in writing. The offer stinks.'

'Thank you. There's one other thing.' He was thinking now of Janie who was ignorant of all this. 'What are Collins's chances of getting away with it?'

'Fifty-fifty at best. I understand he's

fairly new to the game. That being so, he should go cautiously. Be ambitious, yes, but don't let ambition run riot. My source of information thinks Collins is riding for a fall.'

'Will he be wiped out? He has two sons involved with him.'

'You know that, do you? Yes, they'll be wiped out. Not entirely. I am watching Collins. He has a little bit of money hidden away in his wife's name. Not a lot but I'm watching it. I think he realises he may be in trouble, and he is buying himself a bit of security. It's all legal at the moment. It's when he starts to raise money from outsiders that I worry. He can't go public — they'd never accept him as a public company. Not yet anyway. On the other hand he might take in partners — and 'take in' is the operative phrase. He'll take them in, in more senses than one.'

'Got it.'

'Well, here it is in writing, but not nearly as detailed as this talk. It's as non-committal as I can make it. It is unsigned and it wasn't typed here. You can't trace it to me. I have to be careful, even although I've only told you the truth.'

'Thank you.'

Roy took the plain envelope and put it in his pocket, and handed over his cheque for fifty pounds. Laurie Lane mean-time had begun to take books out of the box and was exclaiming in pleasure.

'I love new books. They have a feel all of their own. Mance's produce nicely printed and bound books, don't you think? Ah the cheque. Thank you. Why not come for a stroll in the garden, then we'll have a drink, and then lunch. It's far too nice to stay indoors. I've ordered a cold buffet on the patio for one o'clock.'

It was a pleasant day and Roy left at three, feeling pleased with progress. The next problem was what to do about Janie. Back at the cottage he sat down at his typewriter and broke open a new ream of paper. He made one carbon of his report which he wrote in narrative form; all about his visit to Lane and what had been said exactly as it had been said. It was a very detailed account of his meeting with Lane. To it he attached Lane's written report which was much shorter, and merely outlined the financial structure of Scotland's Panorama and what possible advantage there could be in offering shares to acquire another (unspecified) property.

It was pretty damning stuff, Roy thought, considering that Janie had just got herself engaged to Chris Collins. Perhaps he was wrong. But how could he be? It *had* to be Jack Lyon they were after.

He felt rather sad about it. What would Janie think of it all? What seemed like a generous offer to her father was really a very underhand way of raising money on her father's property.

Oh well, he decided as he got up and took a can of bitter lemon from the refrigerator, maybe Jack Lyon had never intended to go into partnership with Collins anyway. He hoped not.

# 10

On that same Saturday Janie was wrestling with a problem. She had arranged to return to Switzerland early the following week. Chris was persistently trying to persuade her to stay for at least another ten days, and it was difficult to refuse. He had changed a lot, drank far less, and indeed she never saw him drinking although she could still smell it from time to time. He had also stopped smoking cigars in front of her. Again, she knew he did it elsewhere because of the smell, which was rather nice of him. He knew she didn't like it, and so he spared her. He was much more his old familiar self, although sometimes he seemed like a stranger. From the way he talked she had come to the conclusion that he was as hard-headed and possibly hard-hearted as his father. He put his request so reasonably and it was true that another ten days would make no difference to her.

In addition she was waiting word from her father about the deal with Walter Collins. She had a feeling that she might be useful to Jack, here on the spot. She didn't see how, but the feeling was persistent. Yet she was not happy She really wanted to go home.

The hotel was very busy, crowded, and Chris did not have much time to himself. She had to admit that he made a good hotel manager. He seemed to know every detail that was going on, even in the kitchen where he was an intruder unless invited. Nothing was too much trouble for him and his manner with guests was good. He had so many good points to his character.

She was still in a state of chronic indecision when a receptionist came to her room with a slip of paper.

'You have a telegram Miss Lyon. It has just been telephoned through. The confirmation copy is coming later. I thought it looked urgent.'

'Thank you. Thank you very much.'
She smiled at him and the young man's
heart flipped. He wished he had a girl
like her.

She waited till he had gone before
looking at the paper. It was short and to
the point.

'Arriving by road tomorrow. Must
talk about Scotland's view. Hold everything.'

It was unsigned. Clever Roy, she
thought. Scotland's view was Panorama
of course. So he had found out
something and the 'hold everything'
was ominous. She decided not to waste
any time. She went straight down to
reception.

'Can you please send a telegram to
my father in Switzerland for me? Over
the telephone?'

'Of course Miss Lyon.'

'I've written it out.'

It was a short message to Jack. It
read simply 'No deal at any price
report follows'. The receptionist looked

up at her, grinned and picked up the telephone. A few minutes later the message was on its way to Switzerland at full rate and Janie went back to her room again. She had been impulsive but Roy's telegram suggested trouble. It was better to make sure Jack would do nothing than to leave things to chance. After all, if she was mistaken, no real harm would be done this way.

She got out her books and her big loose-leaf ring book, and began to work on some more translating. It took her mind off other things. Chris found her hard at it at ten-thirty. 'Hullo darling, that's no way to spend Saturday night,' he said when he had kissed her.

'What's Saturday got to do with it?' she asked amused. 'I don't work in a factory.'

He flashed her a white smile. 'Then guess what? I, who am a slave to the time-machine, have a whole day off tomorrow. What shall we do?'

'How did you get a day off?'

'I'm taking it. I have a perfectly

capable assistant and it's time he showed his mettle. It so happens that for once we have hardly anyone leaving on a Sunday. Next Saturday and Sunday will be chaos. This week-end is just a freak, and I intend to make the most of it. What shall we do?'

'What is there to do?'

'That sounds terribly cynical. Have you done it all already?'

'We went to Loch Ness on Wednesday,' she reminded him.

'So we did. Let's set off early and visit Perth for the day?'

'All right but I'd like to get back by tea-time.'

'Why?'

'I have a visitor. Roy Monro is coming up to see me.'

'What?' Chris looked astonished. 'He's not booked in. I've just been checking reservations.'

'Perhaps he is booked in somewhere else. Anyway he said he'd be here to see me tomorrow, so I must be back by tea-time. I don't think he's likely to arrive before then but I'll leave word in reception anyway.'

'What's he coming for?'

'A little bit of business to do with translating,' she lied. 'I had some queries and he decided to come up here.'

'What, just to answer some queries?'

It sounded weak, she agreed privately, but she smiled confidently.

'You don't know much about translating, do you?'

'I thought you'd done his book and finished with it.'

'Ah yes, in German,' she said meaningly and he shrugged.

'I don't understand. All right, we'll be back by tea-time. I wonder where he is staying?'

'I suppose it wouldn't be hard to find out,' she said, 'but why the interest?'

'Interest? I'm not in the least interested.' He was needled.

'Sorry. We were talking about tomorrow. We'll go to Perth, shall we?'

'If you want.'

'Look Chris, it was your idea. You invited me. It isn't a question of 'if I want', is it?'

'No. I'm sorry darling,' he apologised again. 'Any news from your father today?'

'About what?' she asked looking blank.

'You know, about that business proposition.'

'There's hardly been time for a reply. Anyway he won't write to me I'm sure. He'll write to your father. I know nothing about these things.'

'Coming down to the bar for a nightcap?'

She went down with him and they had a drink together before going to bed. Next day Chris and she set off by road for Perth, lunched there, walked round the city, and then drove back. It made a pleasant change and the scenery between Perth and Grantown was superb.

'You haven't said anything about your stay,' he reminded her when they returned. They were sitting in the car, in the car park. 'Will you stay for another ten days or two weeks, Janie?'

'I'll let you know in the morning.'

'Mysterious,' he remarked.

'No, but I haven't made up my mind.'

'What's to decide, darling?' he asked. 'It seems straightforward enough to me.'

'What's the point in staying?' she asked. 'You're busy at this time of year. I'm occupying space that could be let to a paying guest. It isn't as though we will never see each other again.'

'You're the girl I'm going to marry,' he reminded her. 'That's the point in your staying so far as I am concerned.'

'I still think I should go home.'

'Had enough?'

'Not in the way you're implying, Chris. I am a little bit homesick, though. I've been away for over a month. That's a long time.'

'We're going to be separated for longer than that, aren't we?' he asked.

'Not a very amusing prospect.'

'It wouldn't be so bad if you were on holiday,' she countered. 'It's frustrating when you're working and I'm not.' It wasn't quite true. She wasn't in the least frustrated. Just homesick.

'I wish I could persuade you. Now that your leg is back to normal couldn't you go for walks. What about pony trekking?'

'Not on my own. I'm not in the mood.'

'I never thought of you as moody,' he told her and she had to admit he had a point there. She was moody and it was unusual. Things weren't working out as they ought to have done.

As they walked towards the front door of the hotel she noticed Roy's car parked near the entrance, in one of the parking spaces.

'Roy's here,' she said automatically. 'That's his car there.'

'Oh. Well I'd better keep out of the way. You'll have things to talk about.'

'That's right. I'll see you later on Chris.'

She ran inside ahead of him. Roy was in the lounge and stood up when he saw her. His eyes lit up with pleasure, and it was a pleasure she shared. He was reassuring, dependable. He looked at her admiringly.

'Hullo Janie.'

'Hullo Roy.'

'Where can we talk?' he asked. 'I've got some confidential stuff for you.'

'There's the writing-room. It's hardly ever used and not on a Sunday evening I imagine. Did you have a terrible journey?'

'Tiring. I slept at a rotten hotel last night and started off again early this morning. I'm whacked.'

'Oh Roy, I'm sorry.'

'No need to be,' he laughed. 'It was all my own idea. I could have posted this to you but it's strong stuff.'

They went into the deserted writing-room and sat down by a window and he told her all that had happened.

'It's all in here,' he concluded, handing her the envelope. 'All of it. Tell me one thing. Is Collins trying to do a deal with your father?'

'You guessed?'

'At first it was a guess, but when I knew Scotland's Panorama were making the offer, and that Walter Collins owns the company, then I knew it had to be that way. I'm sorry about this Janie. I hope you won't hold it against Chris. Walter is just business mad. He's unable to resist a deal. And of course he could make the Lyon family rich.'

'He could also ruin us. What makes me angry is that he talks about the family, as though he were doing the decent thing. He could have spared me that. He could have put it as a straight business proposition. Then if we'd made a mistake it would have been our own fault. Business is business as they say. He's bringing personalities and relationships into it. That's a dirty trick.'

'Well,' Roy confessed, 'I must say that I thought about it a lot during the drive up and it seemed like a pretty dirty trick to me. I repeat, you mustn't blame Chris. No harm has been done. You'll have to tell your father some of this of course.'

'I'll tell him everything.'

'Can't you soften it a bit? You don't want ill feeling between your father and Chris's.'

'I don't,' she agreed, 'but I don't see how I can avoid it. I shall have to have a talk with Chris. This changes things.'

'You mustn't quarrel with him.' He was anxious about her happiness.

'No, but I don't want him to be a part of all this risky dealing. Not now. Whatever Walter has to do to become rich, let him do it alone. I shall ask Chris to come to live in Switzerland. Jack would give him a job in the hotel. He'd be one of us, one of the team. Later on, when Walter retires, he can leave a share in the Scottish company to Chris and we'll see about that then.'

'It sounds fabulous,' Roy laughed, 'but will Chris agree?'

'Why not? Jack wanted someone to

join in with him. It could have been me. Now it can be Chris *and* me.'

'I repeat, it sounds great. What wouldn't I give to be able to come to Lenk to live?' He grinned ruefully. 'The only thing is that Chris may not see it that way. You'll have your work cut out.'

'He loves me. I'll give him that. He does.'

'I should damned well think so,' Roy said flatly.

'Oh Roy, I'm sorry. You still feel the same way?'

He gave her a puzzled look. 'Of course I do. It wasn't a boyish crush, Janie. It is the real thing. It is astonishing, and I don't want to embarrass you by talking about it, but get it into that pretty head of yours that I shall always love you. That isn't going to change.'

'You can't be sure.'

'I can't prove it,' he admitted, 'but I know it, deep inside. That's how it is going to be. It isn't a matter of choice. I'm stuck with it. Now we'd better change the subject. I did promise you not to refer to it again. About Chris, go gently. He may need persuading.'

'He will. He admires his father and thinks he's terribly clever.'

'That in itself is a change nowadays. I thought the majority of young people despised their parents, or at best thought them fools.' Roy smiled.

'No, but I know what you mean. Chris is rather touching about his parents.'

'Good. Well I'd better go.'

'Where are you staying?'

'MacKinnon's boarding house in the middle of town. It's all right. They're arranging a nice hot meal for me now, and I'm having a bath and going to bed early. I honestly thought it better to come up to see you and make the report in person.'

'I understand,' she smiled. She touched his hand hesitantly. 'You've been kind. I had no right to come to you.'

'Oh no Janie.' He stood up, a tall,

broad man in his khaki trousers and black sweater, very slim waisted, rather youthful. 'You're wrong my dear. You always have the right to come to me. I remember an old novel of Maurice Walsh's. It was called *The Key Above The Door*. There's always a key above my door Janie. Come to me any time you need help or advice. I couldn't do less. I'd love to do more.'

'Shall I see you tomorrow?' she asked.

'Is it wise? What about Chris? I tell you what, I'll have a little jaunt about town in the morning, lunch early at MacKinnon's, and set off south some time in the afternoon. I'll take it slowly on the way back. Come and see me if you have time, but only if you want to. I'm not expecting you.'

'It's so unfair, a short meeting like this.'

'You didn't ask me to drive up to Scotland Janie, did you? I came of my own free will. For God's sake keep Jack's money safe.'

'I have done. I've spiked any deal. I'm sure of that.'

'Good girl. You needn't tell your father of my part in this. He might not like me knowing about his business affairs. Just tell him you wrote to Laurie Lane — the chap who writes those books about rackets. After all, that's where the advice comes from although nobody can prove it. He never signs anything, clever man.'

'I shall tell Jack just what I did, and what you did. I've nothing to conceal.'

'I don't suppose it matters. Have a good journey home. You leave soon don't you?'

'I shall leave on Tuesday now. I hadn't decided but I think I'll go. I'll telephone about the car tomorrow.'

'Well.' He held out his hand and she took it. He gave her a funny twisted smile. 'Good luck Janie. I'm glad if I helped. Let me know when you marry, won't you?'

She bit her lip and said nothing as he turned and left the room. When she sat down she had to fight to keep back a few tears. It was really rather ridiculous she thought. Then she tried to concentrate on Chris.

\* \* \*

Chris stared at her. 'I don't understand what you are getting at Janie,' he said patiently.

'I want you to come to Switzerland.'

'But why?'

'Because I want to live there for as long as I can. Later when your father retires you can come back to Scotland if you want.'

'Just like that? You think my father will keep a place in the business for me so that I can have an indefinite holiday in Switzerland?'

'Not a holiday darling,' she said with a sigh. 'You'd help Jack and me with the hotel. He's got plans to build up the business, have more rooms, some shops, I told you all about it.'

'What about *him* going in with *my* father?'

265

'I don't think he'll agree. Forget about that.'

'Oh.' He gave her a funny look. 'That's off? You've had no mail today.'

'I didn't say I had.'

'Then why the change of attitude? How come you suddenly know your father will turn down what must be about the best offer he'll ever get.'

'Is it?'

'Is what?' he queried irritably.

'Is it such a good offer? There's no cash attached to it.'

'Just a great block of shares in a growing company.'

'Never mind that,' she said hastily not wishing to be drawn into a discussion. 'I want to go home Chris. I'm leaving on Tuesday. Why can't you follow me out to Lenk and live with us? Your father can spare you. There's Ian.'

'What about our house in Carrbridge?'

'You haven't settled anything. We've got a nice place to live in Lenk. We could have two or three rooms to ourselves. Perhaps Jack will build us a little place of our own.'

'I don't get it Janie. Have you gone mad? It's the *other way round*. Your father has a chance to come in with us in a really big fast-growing business. I'm not pulling out to bury myself in Lenk.'

'But I want you to, Chris. To please me.'

'It's my career,' he explained impatiently. 'What about that?'

'Oh Chris, do you really mean that? You know as well as I do that your father's little empire is a cardboard one. It could collapse. You don't have a career yet.'

'Yes?' he said, sitting down suddenly and giving her a sharp scrutiny. 'Who says so?'

'You've told me yourself, about borrowing money.'

'For business expansion.' He was watching her closely. 'That's routine. What's all this about a cardboard empire?'

'You know your father hasn't enough

capital, that he's working on mortgages and loans.'

'That again is business practice.'

'If it is properly supported, yes,' she sighed. 'If the banks foreclosed, your father would lose even what he had to start with. Anyway won't you do it to please me Chris?'

'This has something to do with Monro.'

'What?' She gaped.

'Everything was fine until Monro came. Now, an hour after he's gone, you want me to give up and come in with you in Switzerland. He's mixed up in this.'

'How can he be?' she prevaricated. 'He's an author.'

'Rather a crafty one, I suspect.'

'Leave Roy out of this. He's *not* involved. I'm asking you quite simply to give up here and come to Lenk with us.'

'The answer is no, Janie. What's more, this is too sudden. You've never hinted at anything even remotely like it before. I'm suspicious. If not Monro, what? What brought this on?'

'I've just been thinking, that's all. You've been on at me about extending my stay. Well, there's my answer,' she said firmly.

'Just like that. An ultimatum. We were only engaged a matter of days ago. Why did you say nothing then?'

'I hadn't thought about it,' she answered uneasily.

'No, I know you hadn't. It's why you think about it now that puzzles me. All right Janie, go on Tuesday if you want. Perhaps that will be best. However we are getting married next year, and when the honeymoon is over you and I will live in Carrbridge.'

'Is that your last word?' she asked.

'It's what we arranged. I'm not changing. I'm keeping my promises.'

'It isn't a matter of promises. I want to live at home.'

'I want to live here. It's my responsibility to provide for you. If you won't accept the home I provide, there's not much point in getting married.'

'Backing out?' she demanded.

He stepped towards her, hands out. 'No darling. Just trying to make you see it sensibly. You're overwrought. I'll leave you now. See you in the morning. Meet me for breakfast at eight.'

She stood silently as he left. Outside he paused in the corridor and his face darkened. Something had gone wrong all right. He would have sworn that she was on their side, and his father had made it clear that Jack Lyon's money would be a godsend. They might manage without it, but it would be a damned sight easier to manage with it.

Somebody had thrown a spanner in the works. With almost feminine intuition he recognised an enemy in Roy Monro, although Roy had given him no cause to believe this.

He went to reception and told the receptionist to telephone around town to find out where Mr. Monro was staying. It took ten minutes to discover that he was at the boarding house. Chris got into his car and set off for the middle of the town, and parked in the road. He walked to the door and pressed the bell. A few minutes later he was shown up to Roy's room on the first floor front.

'Roy Monro?' he asked, recognising him from photographs on the dust jackets of his books.

Roy nodded. He guessed who his visitor was. It had to be Chris Collins. Who else would call? And anyway the description tallied.

'Collins is my name.'

'Sit down.' Roy was affable. 'You're Janie's fiancé.'

'I'll stand Mr. Monro. Yes, Janie and I are engaged. We don't need any help or advice from you.'

'I'm sure you don't. Is that what you came to tell me?' Roy felt cool.

'Yes.' Chris flexed his muscles as he spoke but Roy was unimpressed. Physical bulk had never cowed him.

'Perhaps you'd explain.' He sat back and crossed his legs.

'I don't know what your game is

Monro, but I want you to keep away from my fiance. Just leave her alone, understand? Otherwise it will be worse for you.'

'How very melodramatic. I'm sure you never read a cheap line like that in one of my books.' Roy could be sarcastic when he felt like it.

'I've more to do with my time. I'm serious. You saw Janie today and you've put some wild idea into her head that she'd be happier in Switzerland than Scotland. I also suspect you've been saying some slanderous things about my father's business ventures.'

'What on earth do I know about your father's business ventures here in Scotland?' Roy asked innocently.

'I'd give a lot to find out the answer to that one. Now, I don't know what you are up to and I don't much care, just so long as you get out of town and get out of our lives. I'm not married to Janie yet, but we *are* engaged. Get out Mr. Monro. Keep away from her.'

'Oddly enough that's just what I'm doing. You didn't need to come here to tell me.'

'Why did you come to Grantown?'

'You'll have to ask Janie. It was on her business, and I'm not prepared to discuss it.'

'I ought to give it to you,' Chris growled, bunching his right fist and making a face.

'Grow up, Collins. You aren't at your expensive prep school now, bullying younger boys.'

'I did not,' Chris flashed.

'Then don't start now. It won't work!'

'You've been warned. Keep away. I mean it.'

'It's up to Janie, not to you. I've no intention of interfering in her marriage, if that is what is worrying you. I haven't tried to.'

'No? Do you expect me to believe that?'

'I don't see why not. I've no interest in her relationship with you. None at

273

all. What's more,' he added taking pity on the younger man, 'I have no intention of seeing her again. I told you, I'm leaving tomorrow. I came here on her private business, and it is finished.'

'All right.' Chris turned and stamped out of the room, feeling rather foolish. He went out and stood in the drive, fuming. He didn't trust Monro. He didn't like him. The man was an obvious menace, although he still did not quite see in what way.

Then he did something childish and stupid. Instead of going out to the street he turned and went round to the back of the house. There was a sort of yard with half a dozen cars parked in it. He found Roy's almost at once, for Janie had pointed it out to him at the hotel and it was the only one of that make and colour there. He looked it over. The petrol cap was a locking one so he couldn't cram earth into it. What else? A potato in the exhaust was guaranteed to provide fun, but first you had to get your potato. He looked for stones but could see none. Then a more interesting thought occurred to him. He went to his own car and took an adjustable spanner and a pair of pliers from the boot. He walked back silently to the rear of the boarding house and lay down under the bonnet of Roy's car. Silently he loosened the track rods and left them holding by only a few threads. Somewhere between here and the Malverns, the steering would pack up and that would give Roy something to worry about. Serve him right if he went off the road and smashed up his car.

Still fuming and smarting Chris went back to his own car and drove to the hotel. He went into the bar and ordered a large whisky, and then another. The barman was expression-less.

'Been in an accident sir?' he asked.

'What?'

'You've got dirt on the back of your jacket, sir, and on the sleeves.'

'Oh have I? I slipped and fell. I didn't

do any damage. Let's have another. Large.'

The barman poured a third and moved away to attend to a hotel guest. He had never liked the boss's son much.

# 11

Chris was silent at breakfast next morning and Janie did not raise the question of their future again. She wanted to get away, to sit down quietly at home and think about it all. Her feelings towards Chris had undergone a change that was no longer subtle. It was becoming too obvious. The question now was did she want to marry him at all? It seemed such a short time since she had arrived in Scotland so full of hope, happy, eager to see him. Nothing had gone well, not a single thing.

She was surprised later in the morning when Walter Collins arrived at the hotel. He came to see her in her room.

'I came at once Janie. I've just had an extraordinary cable from your father. It says quite simply, 'Not interested in any deals.' Now I find that hard to

277

understand. Chris says you are going back soon.'

'Yes I am.'

'Then you'll be able to talk to him, make him see sense. I don't think he realises how much we want him in the business, to make it all one big happy family.' He made an expansive gesture with his hands. 'That's the way it ought to be. You did write about my offer, didn't you?'

'Yes. He should have it. I sent it by airmail right away.'

'Then how do you explain this cable?'

'I can't,' she answered calmly.

'Is something wrong between you and Chris?' he asked.

'Why?' she countered.

'He seems a bit out of sorts. Not his usual self.'

'I suggested that he come out to Switzerland and live with us at Lenk for a few years, and that we reconsider everything later on.'

'Is that what you told your father?' he exploded.

'No it isn't. It was something I thought about yesterday. I miss home, I want to go back.'

'Well that's natural, but Chris will give you a lovely home of your own here in the Highlands. That's a boy with a future Janie. You can't seriously want him to bury himself in a little place like Lenk. It's fine for a fortnight's skiing, but nothing else. Even your father only went there for his health.'

'My father loves Lenk. So do I.'

'All right, all right. No wonder Chris is upset. You say your father knows nothing about this?'

'It only came up yesterday. I sent him your offer, just as you explained it to me.'

'Then it is something else. Now I want you to do something Janie. You get back to Lenk just as soon as you want to go and you explain to that stubborn father of yours just how good it would be, not only for you and Chris but for him too, if the family interests merge. He's got a nice little property there and we ought to do something about it. I'm counting on you.'

'Oh,' she replied miserably. She hated confrontations.

'You don't sound very enthusiastic.'

'I don't think I ought to interfere in my father's business.'

'Come along now Janie, we both know better than that. You've talked to Chris and to me, which he hasn't done. You know what sort of people we are, what we want to accomplish. We want him with us. He's a clever man. He ran his own factory before he went into the hotel business, learning it all from the beginning. I want to work with him.'

'I'll tell him when I get home.' She hated the prevarication.

'That's better, and you'd better patch it up with Chris. He's got to stay here. You must see that. Chris is needed here and this is where the future lies. Wait till he comes out to see you, with photographs of the house he'll buy. We'll have it decorated and furnished exactly as you want. Not many young brides get the chance to start off so well.'

'Thank you.'

'That's my girl. You and I understand one another. If only your father were here I could talk it over with him. Anyway I'll be out at Lenk this winter. Meantime you do all the good work you can. It will be okay in the end. You'll see.'

'Yes Mr. Collins.'

'Dad. I want you to call me Dad.'

She shuddered. She had never called her own father 'Dad'. She didn't like the word. She smiled wanly and he left her. She had arranged to leave the following morning and now she felt anxious to get away. She thought of going to visit Roy in Malvern, for she would like to see him, to be reassured by his presence, but she decided against it. She had taken too much advantage of Roy's good nature already. She spent a miserable couple of hours in her room, trying unsuccessfully to do a little work before having lunch. She went out for a short walk afterwards and when she came back Chris was waiting for her.

'Can we have a talk?' he asked.

She nodded and they went into his office on the ground floor.

'Look Janie, my father told me about your father's cable. Are you sure you aren't trying to sabotage our plans?'

'Sabotage plans?' She looked at him objectively, not quite liking what she saw.

'How can I do that? I thought it was a friendly family offer, not a big financial deal.'

'It's not a big financial deal,' he laughed. 'One medium sized hotel in Lenk. The world isn't going to stop.'

'Listen Chris your father asked me if mine knew about my suggestion that you come to Lenk. He doesn't. Is that clear? He knows nothing about it. I didn't know he was going to cable your father like that.'

'All right, sorry I asked. Anyway everything is all right between us, isn't it? After all, we aren't involved.'

'Aren't we?' she sighed. 'Sometimes it looks like it. I don't want to come to Scotland Chris. Perhaps we'd better break off the engagement.'

'What?' He jumped to his feet. 'Oh no you don't. You promised.'

'That doesn't sound very loving,' she answered with a shaky laugh.

'You're not squirming out like that. It's that blasted man Monro again. Well I fixed him all right.'

'What do you mean you fixed him all right?' she asked scornfully. 'Roy Monro has nothing to do with your family dealings. You can't harm him. He's a writer.'

'He's a driver too,' Chris chuckled unguardedly.

'What have you done?' Janie asked quick as a flash. 'Tell me.'

'Oh nothing.' He realised he was shooting off his mouth.

'What have you done Chris?'

'Nothing I tell you.'

'You're a liar.'

'That's a nice thing to say,' he complained.

'I should have seen through you a long time ago, shouldn't I?' she asked half to herself. 'You're not what I thought you were or even what you pretended to be. I don't even like you any more. What did you do to Roy Monro's car?'

'Nothing. What could I do to it? You think I let down his tyres?'

'Have you been to see him?' she asked suddenly. 'Did you go to the boarding house?'

'Yes but I didn't let down his tyres,' Chris said with a sneer. 'The bloody man is all right.'

'Why did you go to see him? When?'

'I went round there last night if you must know, after our talk, and told him to keep his nose out of our affairs.'

'You did what . . . ?' She was astonished. 'How dare you? He's my friend, not yours. What right have you got to go and talk to him like that? Well I'm sorry Chris. That does it. I'm no longer engaged to you. Here's your ring. Keep it.'

She pulled it off her finger and held it out. He moved back away from it so she dropped it into a letter tray where it lay winking at them.

'I'll leave a note for your father and mother.'

'Oh God Janie.' He grabbed her arm. 'This is a stupid quarrel. Can't we turn back the clock just forty-eight hours to when everything was all right?'

'I'm sorry, Chris, but no. You might as well hear the truth. I had a private investigation made into your company, this Panorama thing. I know all about it. I know your father is desperately short of cash and that he has no more security to put up at the banks, and that that is why he wants my father's hotel. I know all about you. I sent my father a cable telling him to make no sort of deal under any circumstances. I lied about that. Or anyway I deceived you. It's all over Chris. I thought it was just your father carried away by his ambition, but you're involved too. *You're like he is.* I'm sorry but that's the end. I'm not marrying you.'

He stepped back and his hand went up. He hit her backhanded across the mouth and she staggered. Her face went numb. When she put her hand up it came away with blood on it.

'You . . . ' He snarled at her, seeking a word. 'You dared to investigate us? Who the hell do you think you are? I'll ruin your hotel in Lenk. You'll get no more custom from us or any of our friends.'

He was scarlet with rage. She pushed past him, panic stricken, and ran out into the corridor. When she got to her room and looked in the mirror she could hardly believe her eyes. Her mouth was puffed and swollen, and the bottom lip was cut. She looked awful. She sat down on the bed and began to cry.

★ ★ ★

It was a little time before she began to wonder again about Roy's car. She was almost certain from what Chris had let drop that he had interfered with it in some way. She put a scarf round her lower face, and went out of the hotel. It did not take long to find the boarding house. She rang the door bell and asked for him.

'Mr. Monro? He left early, before lunch,' she was told. 'Are you by any chance a Miss Lyon?'

Janie nodded.

'There's a note for you. Wait there and I'll get it.'

She waited at the door until the woman came back with an envelope and handed it to her.

'Thank you,' Janie said and turned away.

She went to a café, ordered tea, and opened the note.

Dear Janie, [he had written],

I'm leaving before lunch after all. Yesterday evening I had a visit from your Chris who was very angry about your suggestion of him going to Lenk to work in your father's hotel. He seems to think I put you up to it, and he was understandably furious. It seems that although my motives are of the highest I'm not doing you any good at all. I don't want to come between you and the young man your own age you love. So this really is goodbye; but I meant what I said. There will always be a key above my door — or more accurately, I never even lock it. There's nothing worth stealing. So if you're ever in a jam, I'll be glad to help. Otherwise I'd better stay away and not spoil things for you and Chris. I do hope you will be very happy. Later, if you get the chance, explain to him that I never wanted to come between the pair of you. He's a fine youngster and I'm sure everything will be great.

I can't tell you how much it has meant to me knowing you. I'm not unhappy. I always knew a man of 46 and a girl of 21 are too far apart to be anything but passing friends. It's a pity, but there it is. I have so many happy memories. Thanks Janie.

A tear came into her eye. A fine mess she had made of it. Now she had lost him. She couldn't very well go back to him, could she? Sorry I made a mistake? He'd think her a real child then. He thought she was going to be so happy with Chris. He had no idea that it was all over with Chris.

She dried her eyes and wondered again about his car. He'd obviously got away safely. What could Chris have done anyway, apart from something childish like letting down tyres or messing up the windscreen? It must be all right. Yet she felt uneasy still. She had a premonition that all was not well.

She re-read Roy's letter, and asked for more tea. What a mess. More than ever she longed for the security of Lenk, the comforting presence of Jack and Susan, a chance to forget everything that had happened. It would soon be time for skiing again. Of course with that slight disparity in her legs she'd never be a champion again. That was right out. You had to be so absolutely sure-footed on a good down-hill, so exact in your anticipation of every movement, able to pare a tenth of a second off this corner and off that one, by little movements which made a difference of feet; nobody with an infirmity that affected their balance, even slightly, could possibly hope to get up to the necessary standard. There might be as little as two seconds difference between the first and the sixth in a race. But at least she would be able to enjoy herself again, to ski for amusement. She wished she were in the sun and the snow now, away from all this trouble.

Which was unfair to Roy. What had Roy done, after all? She looked at her watch. Where would he be now? A hundred, a hundred and fifty miles away. He should be home tomorrow evening. She had a sudden desire to tell him about Chris and the engagement. She could not explain it, for she had no reason to believe that he would take her seriously. He would think her immature. He was always so conscious of his age, never realising that sometimes she was the same way about hers.

She paid for the teas and left, walking slowly back to the hotel. She had a bath, did some of her packing, changed her mind about leaving a note for Walter Collins who could get Chris's version of the affair from Chris, and had dinner in her room. She slept badly and woke feeling wretched. She finished her packing and had her suitcase taken down-stairs.

Chris came up to her stiffly in reception.

'Everything all right?' he asked in a chilly way. She wished she could hear his tone. She was sure it would reflect his outraged righteousness.

'Thank you.'

'Car here?'

'It's due. I shall wait in the lounge.'

'Have some coffee before you go.'

'No thank you.' She was being as stiff as he was.

'I'll say goodbye. I have to go down to the cellars.'

'Goodbye Chris.'

He looked at her, uncertainty in his eyes for a fleeting moment, and then turned away. She was not sorry to see his back. He had almost nothing to do with the rather nice boy who came to Switzerland skiing.

The car turned up at that point and a few minutes later she was on her way south. London was her destination this time. London Airport and a Swissair flight to Zurich. She spent the entire day wrapped in thought. That evening they stopped at Lancaster, for they were coming back by the West Coast route. In the hotel she spoke to the receptionist after dinner.

'I want to make a telephone call but I'm deaf and cannot use the telephone.

Will you please ring this number and ask for this man. I'll tell you what to say and you can tell me his replies. All right?'

The receptionist was somewhat taken aback but agreed. She tried to telephone Roy not once but seven times. There was no reply. Janie frowned.

'Would you like me to keep trying. I'm on duty till eleven,' the receptionist volunteered.

'Please. I'll sit in the lounge and read till then.'

The girl tried several times more, and had the line checked, but there was definitely no answer. Janie went up to bed disturbed. Of course he might be having a holiday on the way home, stopping off for a day or two at this place and that. He didn't need to go back directly. Her uneasiness returned. It persisted until next morning, and they were on their way south when she scribbled a note on a piece of paper and handed it to the driver. It told him to go to Little Malvern instead of to London.

They arrived in the late afternoon and drove up to the cottage. There was no car in the small garage and the cottage doors were locked. She tried the wooden lintel above the door and found the key. A moment later she was inside. It was plain almost immediately that he had not arrived home. Well, that proved nothing. What was she to do?

In the end she explained to the driver that she had to see her friend and that she would spend the night in the cottage, and he could go to a hotel. She gave him some money, and went to the spare room where she unpacked, and then made herself a meal. It was odd being in his house like this. She walked round the rooms fingering things, and even went through his wardrobe and dressing-chest, not looking for anything, merely looking *at* his possessions.

She had a hot bath and went to bed after watching television for an hour or two. She seldom really enjoyed television although she could lip read what people were saying quite well. Rather to her surprise she fell into a deep sleep quite quickly. Somehow her apprehension had faded a little now that she was here at Malvern.

Next day she had another decision to make. She could leave a note, travel to London, and get the first available flight back home. Or else she could stay for another day and satisfy herself that he was all right. Of course, she reminded herself, he might be perfectly all right and not come home for several days. He had no deadline to keep.

In the end she decided to stay. It was a sunny day and she gave the driver a day off while she walked to the nearest shops, did a little shopping, made a salad lunch, and then sat outside with a manuscript she had found on his desk. It was very badly typed, full of mistakes, and covered with corrections in pencil. This must be a first draft or something. She soon became immersed in it.

It was the arrival of his car which finally broke her concentration. She stood up as it crunched over the gravel of the small drive and came to a halt by the door. He stared at her before getting out. 'Hullo Janie.'

'Hullo Roy.'

'Have you been here long?'

'Since last night.'

He frowned and came and sat beside her, leaving his luggage in the car.

'I don't understand. Is something wrong?'

'It's difficult to explain.' Now that he was here, safe and sound, indeed it was hard. 'I had a sort of funny feeling that something might be wrong.' She bit her lip and made a face. 'I may as well tell the truth. I suspected Chris might have done something stupid to your car.'

'What sort of stupid?'

'I don't know. I just thought he might have done something. When I telephoned you the night before last, and you weren't here, I became suspicious so I came here yesterday on my way to London.'

'You telephoned?'

'I got my hotel to keep trying to contact you.'

'I had broken down. I only got as far as Stirling. I was badly held up.'

'What was it?' she demanded.

'Trouble with the tie rods. The steering went completely. Luckily it happened when I was in traffic, moving slowly, and I just mounted a pavement and stopped. I suppose it could have been very serious.'

'So he *did* do something.'

'Chris? Surely not.'

'Was it an accident?' she asked.

'Both tie rods went. As a matter of fact I don't think it was an accident. I may as well confess, Chris and I had a bit of a row. You didn't by any chance get the note I left, did you?'

'Yes.'

'Oh well you know. He left in a temper.'

'He could have killed you.'

'He probably didn't stop to think of that,' Roy answered mildly. There was no sign of the blazing fury that he had felt when he found out what Chris had done, and how near he had been to death.

'You needn't make allowances for him. We had a terrible row. I'm going home. It's all over, Roy.'

'I see. Well, you'd better stay tonight. Haven't you got the car?'

'I told the driver to take the day off and report back tomorrow after breakfast.'

'Perhaps we can get you into a hotel.'

'It doesn't matter. I'll be safe here for one night. I'm quite comfortable in your spare bedroom.'

'If anyone found out . . . ' He stopped and laughed. 'We can talk about that later. I'm going to take my things in, unpack, have a wash, and make a pot of tea. You carry on. What's that you're reading?'

'A manuscript I found on your desk.'

He stood speechless. Changing times indeed. He never allowed anyone to see his manuscripts. Even Gertrude had not been allowed to read them in the rough. She was allowed to see the final typing, when it was all neat and tidy, and that was a concession too, for he really preferred to have people wait till the book was in print. Somehow it didn't bother him, Janie sitting with his latest rough work.

'I hope you can follow it,' was all he said, and he left her to the book.

Not very forthcoming, Janie thought. Did he object to her staying the night? She supposed that he was right, that she should go to the hotel — assuming she could get in at short notice — but it seemed a bit of an upheaval for one night, and anyway she was 21 now. Nobody thought anything about that sort of thing any more.

When Roy eventually returned he was wearing a pair of casual trousers, sandals, and a towelling shirt. He was freshly scrubbed and his hair fell over one eye.

'I feel clean at last. I hate travelling. One always gets filthy. I've got the kettle going for tea. Remind me.'

'I bought some things this morning. You'll find cake and biscuits in the cupboard.'

'That's what I call a model guest.'

He stared at her silently for a moment, smiled abruptly and turned and went in again. When he came back he was carrying a big tray with tea things. He poured and they helped themselves to cake, and he leaned forwards.

'What's this about a row with Chris?'

'It would take too long to explain. The engagement is off.'

'Oh. Just like that?'

'Yes.'

'I'm sorry.'

'Are you?'

'You shouldn't ask me that Janie. I don't like being played with.'

She turned scarlet. She had not been playing with him.

'I hope it wasn't on account of me,' he said.

'Not directly. He was jealous of you of course, and he was sure you had

300

been trying to poison my mind against his father. In the end I became angry and told him I'd had an investigation made into his father's company — I didn't mention your name and I'm sure he never thought of it — and that did it. He was beside himself with rage. I'd already decided I didn't want to marry him. It all went terribly wrong somewhere. I made a stupid mistake.'

'Better to find out now than later.'

'Yes,' she agreed quietly.

'So. And he told you he'd tampered with my car?'

'It slipped out, a suspicious remark. He denied it when I taxed him, but I was certain he'd done something childish.'

'What a lurid imagination you have.'

'What will you do?' she demanded.

'About Chris? Nothing. Let him wonder what happened. I was very lucky, Janie. It could have been very bad. Imagine doing 70 on the motorway when the steering falls apart. It makes you shiver.'

'He must be mad.'

'Pretty angry anyway. Let's forget him. Now about you.'

'I'll stay here Roy. It won't matter.'

'Suit yourself. It's a pleasure so far as I'm concerned. You know that. Is there anything for supper or shall we go out?'

'Let's go to the hotel.'

'The one you stayed in?'

'Why not?' she asked.

'Why not indeed. I'll ring and make sure they can cope with us.'

There was still an awkwardness between them which would not be dispelled. They dined at the hotel, which she had mentioned in a moment of nostalgia because it was so closely linked in her memory with her holiday at Little Malvern. Afterwards they walked back, for she had refused to allow him to drive her, saying she preferred to walk. It was a balmy evening. Automatically they walked on till they came to the lane with the field and the wooden gate, where they had stood once before. That was when he had said he loved her.

Would he ever say it again, she wondered?

They leaned on the gate in the gathering darkness. There was hardly a sound to be heard in the stillness.

'I'll miss you,' he said, looking directly at her. She could just make out his lips.

'Don't,' she answered.

'Sorry.' His head jerked.

'I meant don't *miss me*, silly.'

'What?'

'I may be deaf but you're dumb, Roy Monro.' She smiled broadly.

His mouth was open and he looked rather comical. 'Are you saying . . . ?'

'That I made a mistake about Chris. I'm not going to make another. Yes, I *am* saying. *You* should be doing the saying.'

She was in his arms, and suddenly everything was all right. There were no problems that couldn't be dealt with. This time it was different, this time she knew she had made no mistake. For a long time they stood kissing, and then, silently and happily they walked back.

By the door of the cottage she stopped and took something out of her handbag.

'I might as well keep this, now.'

He grinned. It was the door key.

'Yes,' he agreed. 'You might as well Janie.'

They kissed again and went inside.

## THE END

*Other titles in the*
*Linford Romance Library:*

## SO NEAR TO LOVE

### Gillian Kaye

Despite Emma's dislike of Mr Peirstone, schoolmaster in Ellerdale, she is forced to go to School House to look after his children. There she meets his son, Adam, and falls in love. But Adam's circumstances don't allow for marriage. Then Mr Peirstone dies unexpectedly and Emma goes to work for Dr Redman and his wife, Amy, in Ravendale. The doctor schemes to matchmake Emma and Adam . . . but can there ever be a happy ending for the young couple?